Madsong

Madsong

Serena Sue Hilsinger

Gambit
INCORPORATED
Boston
1970

Lines from "After Great Pain, a Formal Feeling Comes" reprinted
with permission of Little, Brown and Company from *The Complete
Poems of Emily Dickinson*, edited by Thomas H. Johnson.
Lines from "The Straw, the Coal, and the Bean" reprinted with per-
mission of J. B. Lippincott Company from *Fairy Tales of the Brothers
Grimm*, translated by Mrs. Edgar Lucas.

FIRST PRINTING

For Helen Everitt

CONTENTS

*The characters and situations are
fiction. The landscape is real.*

ONE

HALLELUJAH HOLE

Cutting Loose

"Only God knows what will come from such a sky," whispered Stephen, sketching cartoon monsters on the misted window with his finger. Together he and Joy watched the April twilight omen another storm. Uneasiness brooded on the city.

An unseasonable but otherwise natural snowfall was delivered according to prediction. Stephen stayed the night. They went to bed early and next morning awaited the general digging out.

In May the snow disappeared, but cold weather and the uneasiness remained.

"Why not cut and run?" asked Stephen.

Joy could think of no reason.

And so the trip was born—not from a wish to escape the time and place, they convinced themselves, but from a need to stretch, like baffled, cramped animals issuing from hibernation. Stephen was a painter; he needed light. The pall of a winter sky was still stretched over Boston. It was time to cut and run.

Between them they had saved enough for at least a summer of the good life. They bought a '62 grey Falcon station wagon in mint condition from an aged widow who ran it to the market and back on fair days. They gave notice: he to the greeting card company for which he reluctantly worked, she to her public relations firm. They began to dispose of possessions.

Sitting on the floor of her apartment on a Saturday morning, surrounded by piles of winter clothes and two large cardboard boxes labeled CLEAN and SALVA-TION, Joy puzzled over the fate of an unfashionably long but attractively patterned skirt.

Stephen turned away from the window with its grey view to smile at her. "The moulting of the Joy bird."

No, she thought, smiling back, it was a thoroughly human ceremony, the right way to start a life together. Stephen was stocky, but he moved gracefully. He had the smile of an imp but the cheekbones and brow of a god. All in all, it was a noble head. She felt the familiar stinging in her eyes. It was hard to keep the tap turned off these days, so vulnerable was she, so grateful, such a damned emotional fool.

Because it barely fit, she tossed the skirt into the Salvation Army box. Contrary to legends of how it ought to be, love was making her fat not wan. Where would it all end? In obesity, she supposed, and wondered if she would ever again inhabit her old and normal self, the one that often awoke without an appetite—any kind of appetite. Life had become positively Sybaritic, and it was her fault, not his. She knew that Stephen could very well do without . . .

"Boeuf bourguignon. That's what I'll do for dinner. Can we afford a bottle of Pommard, do you think?"

"Darling, it's ten in the morning."

"I know, I know, but as I keep telling you, I am helplessly hungry ALL the time. It's most unnatural. I worry about it, really I do," she laughed.

He crouched down in front of her and cupped her face in his hand.

"Match girl? Are you there? Where's that old inner woebegone? It's the real spirit of the place. You're not to lose it. Hear?" He brushed her forehead with his lips. "Of course we must have wine . . . to celebrate going west . . . the American dream . . . seas of wheat . . . the great golden cornucopia pouring from the sky, purple mountains' majesty, and all the while—America singing. Straight across happiness land. Seventy-millimeter panavision and stereophonic sound."

"That sounds like a different kind of trip from the one I had in mind," she remarked dryly—and regretted it at once. There was an adventure in quicksand around the next conversational corner.

"Unfair. I've given it all up. Grass, speed, snow, and acid. Chemically speaking, I'm a monk in a hair shirt and a brown frock. Will there be anything else, Madam?" He stood and bowed.

Then his voice softened.

"Come on, match girl, I've put childish things away and bid a fond but firm farewell to all the turned-on lads

5

and lasses dancing on the village greens. Metabolism wears down . . . like . . . an . . . old . . . clock." He took a slow, stiff-legged turn around the room—a mechanical toy at the end of its cycle. "The new Stephen revolution is having its day: legality, reality, banality . . . the age of awkwardness—not Aquarius. Betwixt and between, neither here nor there, this boyo is a reasonable dog in a mad sun, not howling . . ."

"Stephen, please land." She examined a sweater for moth holes. "I can't follow you."

"Well then, please pay attention; it's the story of my life. Exactly two months and . . ."—he checked an imaginary watch—"twenty-seven minutes ago, I woke up in a New Haven hospital with a hemorrhage, two broken ribs, a black eye, and no recollection of the events-leading-up-to. At that moment of waking, I ceased to be immortal. It was a most distressing moment, as you may imagine. Since then, I've been straight as lead; I'm my own best angel; I guard myself."

He sank into an armchair, sighing with the weight of the commonplace so that she would laugh. He rarely spoke of the time before they met. When he did, she listened, but kept her questions and her fear to herself.

"I shouldn't be here at all. I should be closed in my garret-like room, producing hallmarks of genius."

"How is Father's Day coming?" she asked sympathetically.

"I'll never make the deadline. They've given me the serious cards this time. I don't mind cartoons or animals, but the straight ones drive me up the wall.

Dad, you may not realize
How very proud and glad
We always are to have someone
Like you to call our dad."

"God, Stephen, what can you do with that?"

"You're a woman, you're the major market, you tell me. How about wild geese rising from bulrushes as an accompaniment. Very masculine. Does it move you to buy?"

"My father doesn't hunt."

Again Stephen recited:

"It's minus the frills and the fuss,
But it's wishing you happiness—plus,
For a day that is swell
And a grand year as well,
With a whole lot of love from us.

For that one I contemplate a ship in a bottle next to an antique globe. What do you think?"

"I pass again," she laughed.

"And then they wrote:

I want to thank you
For your counsel and advice,
Your patient understanding,
Your help and sacrifice
Today and always too,
Because it means the world and all
To have a father like you.

Any suggestion will be gratefully accepted."

"Speaking of fathers," she mused, "I must see mine and tell him we're leaving." Secretly, she suspected that her father didn't really give a damn about the wheres and whens of her coming and going. She was a late and only child. Not innately possessing the skill of fatherhood, he never troubled to acquire it. "Come with me, Stephen," she said on impulse. "Come meet my father."

"Never. Much better to be self-conceived and self-begot like a one-celled thing."

"I almost believe you are. In all these weeks you've never talked about your family. It's a wonder, an unnatural wonder."

Stephen posed as a small boy called upon for a perilous explanation. "My parents: there are two—rich, afflicted with high blood pressure, pyorrhea of the gums, and me. I haven't seen them since my graduation . . . Ah, match girl, there's doubt in your eyes. You don't believe *I* had a graduation."

"I'm finding it difficult, I admit."

"But graduate I did. After eviction from two major universities and a minor college and a few years of irregular and unsuitable employment, I finally finished a course at the Rhode Island School of Design. Ma and Pa were enormously relieved. The sigh heard round the world. Although art was undeniably effeminate, at least it might prove profitable. Visions of cigarette ads danced in their heads. They remembered Norman Rockwell. In honor of my future success they gave me a credit card wherewith to make my meantime way. It was the perfect gift because, what with all the violence abroad and the tremors of cataclysm, I was convinced it was time for a warning—twelve feet high and twenty-five feet wide, but this time not in black and white . . . this time in living color. Before I could paint it, naturally, I needed a war in the flesh and blood. Vietnam was out because my draft board has generously considered me half mad for years. Like the defective and conscientious, I am ruled exempt by the elders. Conveniently, Israel was about to have a war. The credit card got me to Tel Aviv."

He paused, head cocked to one side, awaiting a response from her.

It was impossible to tell his truth from his lie, and Joy knew that Stephen himself was not entirely clear about the distinction at any given moment. Partly true this time, she decided. Curiosity got the best of skepticism and she asked, "What was it like?"

"Tel Aviv? The promised land. Splendidly sunburnt, awesomely arrogant Jews, and everywhere, everywhere, fruit, fruit, fruit."

"The war, I meant, as you very well know."

Abruptly he was serious. "I don't remember it too clearly. There were raids, the war itself, then more raids. They didn't particularly trust American volunteers and there was no time to train me, so they put me on a special detail—burying the enemy. The Syrians sometimes chained their men to the heavy guns. You might think all that went out with Attila. Not true. I got to be very handy with a hacksaw, a specialist at cutting loose. There was one . . . just a kid . . . with an Ali Baba look about him. I swear he was pulling . . . helping me . . . he wanted loose, dead as he was."

"Stephen . . ." she began uncertainly.

"But I haven't finished," he interrupted. "I came back from the war more quickly than I'd anticipated and with

9

no inclination to paint what I'd seen. It was a turbulent flight. All that strapped-in time from Tel Aviv to New York, I saw myself pleasantly following my father. Real estate was a man's estate and a proper fate for a reasonable man. For ten hours real estate was dignity, maturity, security, and I *was* a reasonable man. I disembarked from the plane with one hand clenched, clutching an invisible attaché case from Mark Cross beautifully engraved with my initials in golden Gothic. The vision didn't last beyond the baggage claim, thank God, for there was the impeccable family lawyer to greet me. He took me off for a drink . . . for several drinks. Exit dignity, maturity, security, and real estate; exit the reasonable man. Having discovered hashish and other simple pleasures while warring abroad, I proclaimed their virtues. After our third martini, the impeccable lawyer read me the pure food and drug act, declared me unfit for parental consumption, and rescinded my credit card. Then it all came out. My parents hadn't met me because in my absence they'd both come up with Weak Hearts. The mind boggles at the sheer beauty of the phrase. It astounds me still. Next comes the part reserved for mature audiences only— months and months of bad boyo Stephen exploring pleasures both simple and complicated. Fade-in, fade-out . . . You're squinting and your brow is furrowed. Joy's trying to fact-find."

"How much of it *is* true?" she asked, not expecting an answer.

"Never mind fact." He pulled her to her feet, ran his hands down her body, and kissed her.

"I believe that," she said, "be it fact or fiction."

"Darling woebegone, I love you for saying so."

"You must go," she said firmly.

"Must?"

"Should."

"Tonight, wench, we feast," he growled, then turned to the door, singing:

> "I'm sending these lines today,
> With only one thing to say,
> When we are parted,
> I'm brokenhearted . . .

I have a feeling I'm quitting this job just in time. Imagine being trapped forever in the limerick measure."

"Damned grimy weather," he muttered to himself, trudging down the street. A conspiracy between God and the subordinate creators of air pollution obscured the universe both day and night. Although he liked to amateur in astronomy, he'd sold his small telescope months ago. Not even Palomar could penetrate the steel wool that mantled the city. "Can't think, can't paint, can't breathe."

It wasn't just the weather. He felt that a doorway or the next street might lead inescapably to the strange world he dreamt of and was trying unsuccessfully to paint. On canvas he could get no further than a newsreel view of some well-publicized disaster. It was quite different in his dreams—with a fourth dimensional smell about it . . . perhaps a lingering effect of one of his experiments with drugs. There had been many strange countries in those days.

Now, often there was not just an isolated voice in his head, but an entire chorale, chanting a cappella, like football fans, "Quickly, quickly—time, time." And often he woke with the certainty of harming Joy knocking painfully against his ribs; then, propped on an elbow, he watched, as if guarding her from the intruder in himself, until the rhythm of her sleep quieted him.

He needed a place with a view, good light, and Joy. It was that simple.

Rubbing his eyes to clear his vision, he turned and looked back at the apartment window. She was there, of course . . . just a shadow from his distance. In his mind he detailed her face: very light blue eyes, long dark hair forever escaping order, small sorrow playing here and there.

"Light of my life!" he shouted, and danced a few steps in imitation of the old soft-shoe.

A woman getting out of a cab stared and frowned.

In the long-ledger, her Book of the Known, Joy tried to describe the way Stephen slogged down the street and then turned to dance for her. The long-ledger contained descriptions, memories, and an occasional scrap of verse. Stephen, who disliked dabbling, often asked, "What's the point?"

No point, she thought, turning pages. The long-ledger was an addiction, but a relatively harmless one.

It was all there: a lonely childhood complicated by the early death of her mother, college, three years of nine-to-five in an office where it was commonly agreed that she had a flair for PR, three-week excursions abroad during the summers, and a small but varied procession of men. The list included the bitter black prince of an emergent nation who was studying cunning at a very advanced level, a rather ordinary pacifist from Kansas with whom she declined to emigrate to Canada, and a pure-blooded Navajo interning in gynecology. Now Stephen.

There were, Joy decided, too many lists in the long-ledger. "Why all the catalogues of things?" Stephen once asked, and she had replied with a laugh, "Because they make me feel epical."

Smiling, Joy put the long-ledger aside and closed her eyes to avoid the unsorted clothes on the floor.

There sat Patricia, her cousin, in delicate tweed with a splash of color at the neck. Cousin Patricia was always glamorous, often censorious, and sometimes absurd. Patricia was a stranger but also an intimate, a patron of *New Yorker* ads, an oracle, a kind giver of advice. An imaginary companion since childhood, Patricia now endured as one half of an interior argument between selves.

Turning her head so that the dim grey light might fall more happily upon her elaborate coiffure and elegant bone structure, Cousin Patricia said, "My dear, surely it must be clear to you that this is a mistake. The man isn't stable. In fine, he's daft. Going west . . . what on earth for?"

Cousin Patricia dwindled, leaving behind not a smile, but eyebrows arched in urbane disapproval.

"Stephen isn't daft; he's dedicated and gifted." Joy banished Patricia's eyebrows and saw Stephen's room: the

13

stacks of canvases against the walls and the large abandoned painting on the easel. Stephen said it was necessary to scrap it and begin it again in another place.

"You mistake the boisterousness of that short-legged
creature for panache."

"I love him." For want of something better than a
platitude, Joy tried to bring the conversation to a close.

"Nonsense. You are merely bored," said Patricia from
a great distance.

Ave et Vale

Joy drove slowly past the college buildings and the town square, allowing the house to come gradually into view. Although she seldom visited it now, the house was never far from her mind. The long-ledger was littered with descriptions of its darkly paneled, largely uninhabited rooms. Her childhood was no longer immediate, and the house now bespoke solitude rather than loneliness—a cool, vacant peace. In her dreams it rose endlessly; floor after floor of rooms delightfully beckoned to be discovered. But now, as she approached, it was finite and ordinary: three floors, vintage Victorian.

The house was a period piece and so was her father. The college believed that the preservation of both was its duty. It had leased the house to her father for life.

Her father, who professed Early Romantic Literature, believed only in acts which were ends in themselves. Consequently he was content not to publish his scholarship. He was a respected, tenured failure. Joy vaguely remembered that while her mother was alive there was occasional trouble about his self-contained but fruitless way of life. When her mother died, the trouble ceased. Into that vacuum a succession of housekeepers came and went daily for the days of her youth. She invented Cousin Patricia. Her father taught his classes and in his spare hours withdrew to the minor prophecies of the poet William Blake.

It was impossible to guess what message or what solace he found in Blake, but Blake was his work and his happiness. Joy's own rather limited knowledge of the poet came from a course at the women's college she had attended. A square-jawed female in gabardine bawled three times a week at nine in the morning about the necessity for a liberal point of view when it came to the vagaries of genius. Joy was left with a confused notion that Blake's universe was inhabited by archangels with monstrously large genitals and overlorded by a Creator who punished the meek and rewarded the promiscuous.

Of course, the trouble with her father was not poetry. Nor was it severity or austerity. He was always very nice to her, and his sense of humor was finely honed. The problem was simply his unfortunate, lifelong inclination to forget her existence, while she could never forget his.

She parked the car and confronted the door, uncertain whether to ring or just walk in, for she was not expected. Finally she let herself into the front hall. There she was greeted antagonistically by her Siamese replacements: Urizen, an obstreperous tom whose exploits provided her father with vicarious enjoyment, and Thel, a fixed virgin. From the first landing of the stairway they hissed and spit at her.

It was just like him. Losing his daughter from his house, he promptly negotiated the presence of cats.

He appeared in the upstairs hall and leaned over the mahogany banister, squinting down at her from behind gold-framed glasses, hushing the cats, "Now, now . . ."

"It's just me, father."

"Oh, Joy! There you are!" He hailed her as though she were the disembodied abstraction. It sounded more like a hymn than a hello.

"Have I ever told you how I hate my name? It sets up the most extraordinary expectations in people."

"Yes, yes." Because his voice was so very kind, his indifference lacked sublimity. He padded down the stairs. "What a nice surprise. I was just having my lie-down."

Joy damned herself for forgetting that he rested each afternoon on a doctor's advice. Looking him up and down, she noted the carelessness of the latest housekeeper: his trousers bagged, their crease was almost gone.

His height—six and a half feet—was the truly spectacular thing about him. He stooped, and she kissed him, inhaling the comfortably familiar odor of his shaving cologne. Arm in arm, flanked by the two cats, they walked to his study.

"You've been well, father?"

"Yes, yes. Quite well indeed."

Her eyes accustomed themselves to the room's dark clutter and sought the scroll hanging on the wall, a gift from one of those sallow, intense heroines of his late middle age (they were fewer each year) who worshipped his wisdom on a regular basis, thereby earning high marks and a measure of his aloof affection. The scroll bore the poet's *Proverbs of Hell*. From the first—*In seed time learn, in harvest teach, in winter enjoy*—to the last, Joy's particular favorite—*Enough! or too much*—the proverbs were etched in India ink upon a rolled length of fine bond with all the patient pointillism that a bygone spinster might have devoted to a sampler.

Her father settled himself formally at his desk and said, "Well now, let's have a look at you," as though a full and accurate appraisal of her form and content could be made from no other vantage point.

Joy swept a newspaper from an armchair and wondered at its presence while he examined her.

"You've changed," he mused, "you've . . ."

"Filled out is, I think, the usual expression, father."

"Quite so, filled out. Such an odd phrase." Again he stared at her and added with unexpected approval, "Why you're almost buxom."

To escape further scrutiny she sank into the armchair, pulled her feet up under her, and fanned the folded newspaper.

"Not suddenly keeping up with things, are you, father?" she asked with a grin. His remoteness from the times and customs was an old subject of both humor and contention between them.

"No, you needn't look for the millennium this week. It's the chess column, not the headlines I'm following—a ten-board, double-round match between Russia and

Czechoslovakia. Most exciting. Why just today there's a fascinating refurbishment of that old chestnut, the Budapest Defense . . . Ah, but I'm forgetting that you don't play. You would never learn." His sigh confessed gentle reproach.

"I haven't the head for it, father, you know that. Eternally addled." She tapped her brow, then shook the newspaper at him, chiding, "But at least I try to keep up."

He leaned back, his fingertips touching as if in a gesture of prayer, and regarded the ceiling. "I am reminded of a planetarium."

Joy groaned silently. His classroom manner was on him.

"Events spin round us, vast and indifferent as solar systems. One sits dumbly and uncomfortably in the middle of it all . . ." He lapsed and smiled irrelevantly, as if allowing his imagination a respite from such a grim universe with a quick glimpse of that warm paradise of gay children envisioned by the poet in his ecstasy.

"Where was I?" he asked, fumbling back to the conversation.

Unaccountably annoyed for the moment, Joy snapped, "Some people feel they can't afford the luxury of not keeping up."

He was obviously startled, and she heard the shrillness in her voice, its pointless acerbity. Her regret was immediate; she disliked appearing so graceless before him.

"What a silly thing to have said. I'm sorry, father."

" 'The cut worm forgives the plow,' " he quoted dryly. His hand trembled slightly as he straightened a pile of papers and smoothed the page of an open book. Again he quoted—this time his favorite homily, his apologia: " 'Life is short, art is long.' " Having thus delivered himself, he beamed.

She squelched a giggle. He was so very long himself and always seemed to her more art than life.

"Now then, what have you been up to?"

"The fact of the matter is, I'm in love." She surprised them both with a baldly dramatic contralto and they laughed. "It's difficult to say it straight out like that. One feels such a fool, but there it is, and I'm about to go away with him."

Tolerance was a function of her father's detachment, and censure was not a part of his working vocabulary. However, he was not of, or very knowledgeable about, the Age of the Pill. He glanced surreptitiously at the cat Thel, rubbing herself voluptuously against a chair leg, as if he were thinking it would be a happy thing if spaying were general among all species.

"Where will you go, you and your young man?"

Joy sensed that there would be no further questions. Stephen was to be simply and properly labeled, and so coped with, as her "young man," although for all her father knew he might very well be a boy of twelve or an ancient of seventy-five.

"We'll head west next week."

"The West? How peculiar . . . but then one would expect an old fogey like me to prefer the old world . . . the West . . . One thinks of it all—the country, I mean —sitting behind one, very large and strange, ready to push one into the sea if provoked."

"You're becoming very fanciful lately, father."

"Yes, yes." Again his fingertips achieved the angle of worship and his gaze ascended to the ceiling.

They sat on awhile in comfortable silence, for, if there were no words, there was at least mutual affection and well-wishing.

"You will want to have a look round before you leave," he said finally.

And she did. It was her habit to renew her connection with the house, slowly and alone, whenever she visited. The furnishings were solid and accommodating rather than esoteric and valuable. She strolled from room to room, touching the objects of her oldest love—here a marble tabletop, there the carved dragon on a chest of drawers, until the somber wood, high ceilings, and dark odor of polish seemed again more life than dream. Then she returned to her father in the study.

Courtly but forgetful in his fur-lined slippers, he accompanied her to the car and peered at it fore and aft, for her sake politely pretending a sudden interest in things mechanical.

"It runs well, doesn't it? You've a long way to go."

"Yes, if you speak to it often in soft monosyllables," she replied, catching and holding his hand.

"And this? What is this all about?" he asked. Upon both doors of the car Stephen had painted in small gold letters *RUEFUL HOPE*.

"It's my young man's idea. See here . . ." She pulled him around to the front of the car. "The grill and the headlights—mouth and eyes, a perfect portrait of cheerfulness just on its way down to dismay, and so Stephen calls the car the Rueful Hope."

"Why yes, he's got the expression precisely right—rueful hope." The whimsy delighted him. He repeated it under his breath several times, then opened the car door for her. They kissed, but she was awkward about it, so it was more nearly a collision than an embrace.

"Go forth, go forth," he said with a flourish.

As she drove down the street she saw him in the rearview mirror: a tall figure with a certain frayed elegance.

"Go forth, go forth," he muttered again, with distant love and distant pride; it was all he could do in the way of a blessing. Standing on the curb in his slippers, he dreamt of other matters; he dreamt of a woman.

The heroine of his late middle age was quite beyond his daughter's most extravagant imaginings. She was the widow of a professor of European history. He walked with her each evening when the weather allowed, four times around the town square and an added three-tenths of a mile among the graves behind the Congregational church where squirrels and blackbirds could be observed in abundance and graven ciphers, blunted by time, defied translation. There the widow fecundated the air around them with currents of wit and rich, deep laughter.

In particular, he dreamt of the place between the widow's breasts, a fair valley that held the promise of sweet refuge from the winds of indifference and the glaciers of age. He caught himself humming, "Ah Sweet

Mystery of Life," then laughed at himself, then smiled a secret smile. "Old fool, old fool."

Shading his eyes, he looked down the avenue. The elms formed a perfect arch of green. Spring had finally come. The Rueful Hope was beyond his sight.

3

Journeys Out

They left at nine one morning and shared the wheel in two-hour shifts, driving to the electrified beat and twang of rock. In the long-ledger Joy recorded names with a wobbling hand: *Canajoharie, Skaneateles, Batavia . . . the Led Zeppelin, the Grateful Dead, the Iron Butterfly.*

Stephen confessed in a stage whisper, "I much prefer Miles Davis or Coltrane. That's how old I am."

It was late when they reached Astabula and the stale air, scented toilet paper, and wall-to-wall synthetics of a medium-priced motel.

Flicking on the TV, Stephen shouted to Joy, who was in beautiful pain under a needlepoint shower: "Hey, they're playing ye old assassination-cum-funeral tape again!"

"Oh, turn the hideous thing off!" she shouted back. "I can't bear it again."

24

"What? And miss the drums? And the black horse?"

It was a bad joke, he discovered, turning back to the set. What they were playing wasn't a rerun. This time it was the handsome young Caesar struck down—the one with all the kids.

Later they broke out the fifth bought by Stephen for travel and got a little high waiting for news. They lay in the extra long, extra wide, comfort-guaranteed bed, the room dark, except for the flickering images on the square of grey light. Sometime after two in the morning news of the death was brought to them, along with a ballistics report. It was all over but the burying.

They turned off the set, they reached for each other, they slept, for it had been a long day and, as Stephen said, there wasn't a single thought one could have about the event that wasn't a jingle or a slogan or an arch cliché.

Joy climbed the stairs of the house slowly, one hand running along the curve of the banister. The stairs led, as always, to an open door. It was a music room this time. In one corner there was a clavichord, in another a harp, and displayed in the center of the room, the instruments of a string quartet. She wondered if the concert was about to begin, but when she approached the instruments she saw that someone had been there before her and cut all the strings.

Stephen also climbed the stairs, although he knew very well that they existed only in a facile lithograph on display at a small Boston gallery. The stairs led to a hall of orange, diamond-shaped tiles and a cracked and peeling doorway through which could be seen three other equally decrepit doorways diminishing in the distance. "How cheaply dramatic," said Stephen. "This is ridiculous." He walked to the final doorway but did not look through it.

Instead he awoke to find Joy thrashing about. She seemed at swim in her sleep and she was crying.

"No, you mustn't," he murmured, stroking her forehead. She was damp from fear or some such thing. A dream, he supposed. "Sleep, sleep; sleep quietly, sleep deep." He repeated it again and again, in awe of the trust her helplessness implied. When she seemed to rest more easily, he thought how amazing it was that despite his pretense of skepticism and his desire for tough-mindedness, at heart he remained a child, capable of the most appalling acts of faith; for to be absolutely honest with himself, he really did believe that if they were simply good to one another, if they could just keep that much of it intact, God would reward them in some way. He lived in perpetual fear that his instincts would somehow betray his belief.

He could not sleep. The pulse in his head banged, "No time, no time."

The next morning they moved on, across Ohio, Illinois, Iowa. Joy wrote: *Sandusky, Geneseo, Rock Island. Mare's tails in the sky, but the view from Toledo was smog. Children with a pet owl. A boy spearing carp. A tandem trailer with a sign at its rear: "Don't hump." Telephone poles: so many crosses growing infinitely smaller.*

The radio kept them dismal. The body was being flown back east.

Ourselves from the air: an ant swimming up an artery —against the current.

The Rueful Hope ran roughly at the high speeds of Interstate 80. Joy put the long-ledger aside and watched, from West Liberty to Lambs Grove, the green undulations of the land. Her attention soon flagged, her mind took a sudden turning, and Cousin Patricia, indefatigable in Liberty lawn, sat composedly in the back seat, remarking, "Deserts of vast fertility." Then she faded. Joy repeated the remark for Stephen's benefit, adding, "I don't suppose it's really the fault of the scenery."

"A mood of mild desolation brought on by a national catastrophe," Stephen suggested, humorously but sympathetically. "This trip has turned out to be more than a little black-bordered. The thing for you to do is drive, not think." He pulled off the highway and onto the shoulder. They got out to change places, stretched, yawned, and looked at the view. There were fields, of course, and in the middle of them, one house, one barn, one silo, one vine-covered windmill, and one partly blasted oak. In a yard two pigs, two cows, and a horse shared a trough—for all the world like a children's fable demonstrating the innocence and benevolence of the animal kingdom.

"It makes me nostalgic," said Stephen. "No wonder ninety-nine out of one hundred people believe in reincarnation, whether they admit it or not. I most certainly do. I can see myself a hundred years ago—barefoot, with a distinctly Huckleberry air." He posed, chewing a blade of grass, shouldering an imaginary fishing pole.

"Nonsense, Stephen. You were born decadent—every time."

They drove on, surrendering to the torpor of speed.

In the late afternoon the sky turned rancid and they entered the region of a tornado watch. The emergency was short-lived and the storm passed safely to the north; nevertheless, Joy was sufficiently unnerved by the look of things to ask if they could stop early.

They found a room in a large motel appended to a small town. The number of cocktail lounges and gift shops along the main street testified clearly to the fact that it was a case of the tail wagging the dog.

"God, how I hate rented beds," Joy said as Stephen brought in their suitcases.

"This one's electric and perhaps even orgasmic." He pointed to the wires connecting the bed to a coin-operated massager. "Solo performance." He put in a coin and they watched the bed throb until they collapsed on it with laughter.

"Now, match girl, what this disaster area needs is protein." He sucked in his cheeks—a bad version of undernourishment. "Like knights of old in lands of gold, let's go in quest of a couple of steaks unadulterated by tenderizer. Hope T-bone, girl, pray rare." He pulled her up from the bed.

They found a reasonable cafe and ate overdone steaks in silence, eavesdropping, as they both liked to do, upon the surrounding conversations. Because the cadence of midwestern speech was strange, they could understand little of what was said. After dinner, in the calm before night, they walked the town and found themselves in the center of the place—the square—as darkness settled.

The square was literally that, demarked by two churches, a town hall, and a school. The town hall flag was at half-mast, mourning bells tolled discordantly from one of the churches, and a small memorial service was under way by candlelight on the greensward. Stephen and Joy stood at the edge of the group as the reverend spoke softly of "our brother departed" and implied that death was nonpartisan. Many seemed grieved. One woman wept openly. "The Battle Hymn of the Republic" followed as a matter of course. The first verse went well and lustily, but, that accomplished, there was much awkward uncertainty about the words until the safety of the second chorus was finally reached: "Mine eyes have seen the glory of the coming of the Lord . . ."

"It's a very bad song," Stephen whispered too loudly. "The last thing anyone sane wants is a flat-footed Christ proliferating a lot of wrath."

Joy said nothing, but it seemed to her that as a lullaby it was hardly enough.

When the service was over, they walked silently back to their motel room and, as if hypnotized, turned on the TV and watched more mourning.

"This is absurd," Stephen suddenly said. "I'm going to get some air."

He was gone without looking back before she could say a word.

He bought the last local paper left in a vending machine

and found an almost deserted bar without a TV. Over a beer, he read and reread the front page, as if words could make real what the grey repetition of images could not. Then he began to sketch on a napkin. He hadn't scrapped his unfinished painting. It was carefully stored in cardboard at the back of the Rueful Hope. Now he thought that perhaps the problem with it was its total abstraction. It had no people in it, no living thing. He sketched the candlelit faces of the mourners, but either the design in his head wasn't right for the faces or the faces weren't right for the design in his head. He could see at once that it wouldn't do.

At closing time he walked the length of the town and sat down on a bench on the greensward. Very carefully, he furnished the scene in his mind and put himself into it, and then, over and over again, he took the bullets into his own body, until it was his death too.

It had happened before, his damned moods, his departures. She could only wait it out.

"The artist manqué," sneered Cousin Patricia from an inner chamber, "all temperament and no talent."

Joy fiddled in the long-ledger with a description of the ceremony they'd seen, but she couldn't keep her mind on it. Nor could she concentrate upon the latest collection of a lady poet. The poems were presumably about sex but much too abstruse to dance to. They gave no relief to a mind already deadened by travel and treachery.

She went out to the Hope, lay down on the front seat, and listened to a late night DJ who played quiet crooners instead of rock and rarely interrupted with the news. Old men sang gracefully about love. They seemed to have a great deal of distance on the subject. It was a comfort.

It occurred to her that there was really nothing to prevent her from driving off . . . off into the night, without so much as a good-bye, and so be free of his nonsense . . . off to the west coast—San Francisco—for it was reputed to be a wonderful city . . . see San Francisco and die, people said, or words to that effect . . .

Later she awoke to find Stephen shaking her and the radio still playing.

"You bastard," she said, emerging from sleep. "You fucking, frigging bastard." Having practiced it through a whole album of Sinatra, she was proud of the glib way she handled the alliteration, and so she repeated, "You fucking, frigging bastard."

"Never swear in tautologies, match girl, it deadens the effect."

"I almost drove off without you."

"Your almosting is one of the things I love best about you. It was just a matter of getting some air. Nothing to worry about. Don't grouch at me, don't grudge."

She would not speak to him at first, but later peace was negotiated; territories were annexed.

The next day they crossed Nebraska. It turned unbearably hot. Dust devils rose from the plains and cattle clustered within the scant shadows of windmills. Long brown clouds followed pickup trucks down dirt roads. The Hope overheated.

As station KRNT gave way to station WOW, the body was borne from New York to Washington by train. Along the tracks there were two unnecessary deaths and various off-key versions of farewell played by high school bands.

The same stretch of yellow horizon with muzzy cows seemed to unreel itself forever on the windowshield. "Do you really think we're getting someplace?" Stephen asked suspiciously, reaching for the map. To describe Nebraska, the day, and themselves, Joy wrote in the long-ledger: *Spirit level: flat.* They were tired, not so much from the strain of feeling as from the strain of trying to feel, the strain of attention.

4

Love in a Cabin

The next day the mountain range surprised them, rising suddenly out of the plains like a false facsimile of something read about but never quite believed. Joy was reminded of models made in grammar school, constructed of papier-mâché and painted a blunt purple, in the ever-enduring but usually futile hope of impressing the teacher.

"Olympus, Ararat, Pisgah . . ." Stephen listed. "Surely it behooves us to take mountains seriously."

Three hours later, halfway up a mountain, approaching the continental divide, in the town of Hallelujah Hole, they stopped at a general store advertising in its window: *CABINS FOR RENT*. It was a long time before they could command the attention of the proprietor. He and a truckdriver were involved in the reception and disposition of a small but apparently urgent consignment of

Coors 3.2 beer. After a loud dialogue about orders and shipments, owner and driver finally came to the front of the store. The shopkeeper pulled up his right cuff, exposing eight inches of steel hook, punched the cash register, and dealt change for a five to the driver with flamboyant dexterity.

"Do me a favor, next time don't tell me your troubles. Just get it here on time. If I say Tuesday, I mean Tuesday. Is that so much to ask?"

"OK, Max, OK. Tuesday it is. Oh hey, I almost forgot, I think I spotted a junk for you. It won't cost you a dime. The guy just wants to get rid of it—the sooner, the better. You interested?"

"Yeah, you bet I am." Max shrugged and shook his head gravely. "It slipped another couple of inches last night. In bed, I was. Scared shit out of me, I don't mind telling you. Thought I'd had it for sure. The garage is all the way gone. Since a week ago at least."

The driver slapped Max's shoulder sympathetically and left, nodding in a friendly, curious way to Joy and Stephen.

"All the way gone," muttered Max. "You be sure and give me a call about that junk," he yelled after the driver. "Now, what can I do for you folks?"

"We saw your sign about cabins."

"Yeah. Got two cabins. One stone, one log. Someone's living in the stone, so I can only give you the log. Very clean. You like peace and quiet?"

His tone implied that anyone of sane mind liked peace and quiet. They nodded.

"Then I got the place for you. Best location in the state for peace and quiet."

"How much do you want for it?" Stephen asked.

"For the log?" Max staved off the necessity of an immediate reply with a useless question.

"For the log."

"Seventy-five."

"A month?"

"A month! Whatta you crazy? Seventy-five a week and that includes furniture and linen and utensils."

"Come on, Joy, let's go. Seventy-five a week! Not on your life, you one-armed bandit."

"Ha!" snorted Max. And then he roared his appreciation of Stephen's humor. "You're OK, kid; you're OK. For you maybe I can do something." He thumped Stephen on the back with his hook. "I gotta make a delivery up that way. You and the little lady come on along with me and take a look at the place. If you like it, we'll see what we can do."

"Good enough."

"Not from these parts, are you?" Max put OUT TO LUNCH in the window and removed CABINS FOR RENT.

"No, not from these parts." Stephen did not volunteer any further information.

"Well, I don't hold it against you, because neither am I."

Outside Max eyed the Rueful Hope. "She looks just about ready for my collection."

"She runs better than she looks. What collection?"

"Come around back and I'll show you. Watch your step, little one, it's muddy."

Joy had the feeling she'd just been christened.

They walked around the back of the store and down a ragged path to the river. There Max's collection and grief were explained without a word. His garage had already collapsed into the riverbed, and his small house was dangerously close to the edge of the bank. Nearly a dozen cars in various states of decay bolstered the crumbling bank.

Max stood stock-still with wonder on his face, as if he were contemplating it for the first time—through their eyes.

"A river changing course . . . whoever heard of such a thing? Who would expect such a thing from a river?" His voice clearly implied the utter fecklessness of all things, natural as well as human.

Stephen helped Max load some of the Coors into his I. H. Scout (now *there* was real transportation, Max said), and they followed him up the road in the Hope. As soon as they were alone, Stephen burst out: "I knew it. I knew it as soon as I walked in. I said to myself, Stephen, my boyo, you are about to meet one of the great losers of the world. I somehow could tell from the look of him, that look of stoical expectancy, here was a prototype of the species. Very important losers are, you know —in fact, vital to human security. They act as fate's lightning rods. They attract and absorb most of the demons of perversity so that the ordinary Jack and Jill like you and me can lead ordinary lives protected by big, fluffy, down-filled cushions of statistical probability. One-armed and his house is falling down! When close to him, beware of banana peels. From womb to grave, it's one long mine-field for poor old Max. Imagine living like that."

"You needn't sound so gleeful about it, Stephen." Joy doubted neither the existence of the disease nor that Max was its victim, but she did wonder if the affliction were open to self-diagnosis. Did Max know he was a loser? Was she immune? Was Stephen? She shuddered.

"Did a goose walk over your grave?" Stephen laughed derisively.

The cabin was three miles from Hallelujah Hole and the abandoned gold mine from which the town derived its name, on a mountain surrounded on all sides by higher mountains. It was off the road with a small creek running past it. As they walked to it, Stephen grabbed her arm and pointed up. One peak towered above all the mountains. Its bare stone face caught the sinking sun and glowed—a fiery slab.

"My God!" he whispered.

Ignoring the peak, Joy took in the trees, the rushing water, the cool quiet of the place. "It's lovely," she said.

"You folks take a good long look at the place by your-selves. I'm not going to pressure you. If you like it, un-pack. We'll work something out later. If you don't, leave the key in the lock and go on your way. I got an errand up the road."

"Pretty sure of yourself, aren't you?" Stephen grinned.

"The place sells itself, you'll see."

And it did. There were four large, airy rooms: a kitchen, a front room, and two bedrooms. One of the bedrooms would do perfectly as a studio for Stephen.

"Three walls of windows!" Stephen was ecstatic. The hot late-afternoon sun surrounded them. "Did you ever see such enormous, such practically preternatural, such high, wide, and glorious windows? Of course, the furniture is crude, and there isn't much of it . . ."

"Things can be done, Stephen. Things can be done. It's a small matter of wands, sacred reeds, a spell or two— perhaps even a lamp."

"Yes, we'll have ourselves a lamp and rub it. All will be well."

"I love it, I want to stay," she said, as they surveyed the other bedroom and avoided confronting the fact of the bed. It was more nearly a funnel than a flat surface.

"It will be even better. You'll see, Joy. I'll paint you a ceiling . . ." he pointed to the plaster above the bed, "such as no man or woman has ever seen in chapel or brothel. See there—a circle of countless nymphs oh so gracefully and graciously disrobing, and there—in the center—alone, but perfectly up to the occasion, a satyr of such prodigious potency that you will, by merely looking up at him, conceive giants. Will you have giants? Come here, I will get you a Hercules."

"No giants just yet, you idiot."

"No giants? What a pity. Oh well, come here anyway . . . Now tell me . . ." he preened in a throaty baritone, "am I not the prince?"

"No."

"No? How can you have the audacity to say simply and flatly 'no'?"

"No, and again no. For one thing, even now, after all this time, I don't quite believe in you. For another thing,

you're being good to me . . . you are, Stephen, don't
look away . . . I want to tell you . . . I want you to
know . . . and the prince is never good to the match
girl, not ever. And, for a third thing, you are a bit—just
a bit, mind you—too short, too stocky for the prince.
But princely you are. Yes. Once and forever princely."

"All right, if I'm not the prince, perhaps I'm the frog,
waiting to be kissed."

"Not by me. If this is a spell, I won't be the one to
break it."

"It is a spell—a spell all around us: the frog and the
match girl preserved before their ruin. But not a spell
of cold—no ice palace this. It's a spell of light. We must
have no blinds, no shades, no drapes. Light all around us."

"And at night, Stephen?"

"Not a bulb a watt less than seventy-five. And so, you
see, it's quite safe to kiss the frog."

Later they moved in and dined from a can of salmon Joy
had packed in case of emergency. Stephen set up his
painting things in the spare bedroom, bestowing on
bristles and tubes the lavish care of a voluptuary, and
then watched Joy.

"Joy in a cabin," he said, for she was nesting already;
it was already Darby and Joan. Wherever she was, no
matter how small the space or short the time, she instinctively staked a claim and began to straighten. He
was amused, moved, and annoyed by her domesticity and
took a walk to sort out his feelings.

Jogging down the road, he soon forgot both Joy and
the cabin, for it was a beautiful night. The Andromeda

galaxy could be seen with eyes alone, so clear was the atmosphere, so close the sky.

It was only after he'd run himself out that he realized he was there to keep an appointment. The peak by moonlight was as he expected—cold, forbidding, lovely.

When he got back to the cabin he found Max at the door with the wreck of a handsome woman in tow. She was tall and very thin. Her flesh gave evidence at every juncture of the workings of the skeleton beneath. She wore Wrangler jeans of the stretch variety and a flannel shirt that might have belonged to Max. By a short chain she held a hoary greyhound obviously long since retired from the active life of long shots and mechanical rabbits.

Stephen ushered them in, took the beer and pretzels offered by Max, and called to Joy, "Max has come, bringing a party."

They introduced themselves all around. The wreck and the dog were Selma and Mr. Quick. The dog nuzzled mournfully against his mistress, as if aware that the name so handsome in his sleek and slippery youth was now a sad misnomer.

"I knew you'd stay, kid. I said, 'Selma, we got company for the summer.' Didn't I say that, Selma?"

Selma nodded shyly.

"One hundred and fifty a month and not another word." Max brought his hook down flatly on the makeshift coffee table.

"You've got a deal," Stephen said with alacrity. He'd counted their remaining traveler's checks and knew that was about what they could afford if they were careful about food and drink.

Love in a Cabin

In the absence of glasses they drank from the cans. Max promised an early morning delivery of utensils and dishes. Selma cleared her throat huskily for a toast. "We only pass this way once," she said, "enjoy."

"Enjoy," they all repeated. In Joy, Stephen mouthed silently. It was an old joke between them.

They relaxed into beery conviviality, and soon the conversation became personal. No, they weren't like those kids who made trouble all the time; for one thing they were too old, too old for revolution—and look how clean they were. No, they weren't married.

"That's no one's business, Max," Selma chided. "The arrangements of love are sacred and untouchable."

It developed that Selma, once turned on, was a great talker about life, a rather bardic ruin. She lived a short way up the mountain in Max's stone cabin, alone with the dog whom she'd saved from the pound when his career was ended by age. "I used to go to the dogs a lot," she explained. "As a matter of fact, I'm still going to the dogs." She laughed and laughed. It was a nice let's-all-let-our-hair-down-about-life laugh. Joy and Stephen liked her immediately.

Unfortunately Max caught sight of the painting gear in the adjoining room, and Stephen was forced to confess with a squirm in his voice, "Yes, I paint."

"Well, I'll be. I told you they looked like an interesting couple . . . now, didn't I tell you that, Selma?" Apparently they were tenants to be proud of.

Sensing that Max wanted and waited to be asked, Stephen said, "Tell us about the arm. Accident?"

"Nah. The war." Max leaned forward intently. This was his métier.

The coffee table underwent transmutation—it *was* the Burma road at dusk. Coins from his pocket became encampments of Japs, columns of Yanks.

"And then . . ." Max surveyed his child-eyed audience. "Vah-vah-vah-voom! Right on top of me. Look, Ma, no hand." He waved his hook exuberantly. But explosion and amputation were only penultimate.

"On . . . the day . . . before . . . my furlough." He spaced out the words so that his listeners might steep in the full flavor of his gift for misfortune.

"It was the kind of war where you could sit on your ass in New Zealand for four years, but that's not my kind of luck."

"Max has the Purple Heart." Selma crowned his narration with pride.

"Yeah, yeah," he said deprecatingly. He did have it. With him. He was persuaded to show it around. Stephen examined it seriously, hefted it once or twice, and passed it to Joy. She took it gingerly.

"Whatsa matter, little one, does it spook you?"

"A little," she admitted.

"All water under the dam." He pocketed the medal. "I make out OK. Don't I make out OK, Selma?" He put a lecherous arm around her.

She rose, blushing. "Come on, sweetie, let's let these people get some sleep." At the door she made Joy promise to come up for a visit.

"Take care, Max, take care," Stephen called after him, remembering that the man's house was on the verge of collapse. He watched Mr. Quick lead Selma up a dark path.

"Two losers in one day and one place. Fantastic."

"Are you sure there are only two?"

"Three hundred percent."

Although bone tired, they both slept fitfully. The bed would take some getting used to. Joy dreamt of an enormous room full of beds: four-poster beds, canopied beds, trundle beds, bunk beds, convertible beds, and beds that came out of the wall. All had firm, inviting mattresses.

Stephen dreamt of the peak. When he woke, he remembered the dream and knew he could paint it. He felt that the poison was out, the long months of drugged nightmare finally over. There was Joy and his work. Everything else seemed very far away.

The peace and quiet were not quite as advertised by Max. The beasts of reclamation began to roar at seven in the morning. It was impossible to tell whether the machines were widening the road, narrowing the road, or, as Stephen suggested, merely keeping it the same by moving piles of earth from one side to the other.

Actually Stephen didn't mind the noise. It meant early and easy waking—a full day's work. As soon as Joy left to explore Hallelujah Hole for provisions, he began, covering the old, unfinished canvas with bold, thick strokes of white paint. Such a heavy wash would give the new painting texture. With obliteration came freedom. Whereas before the lines were thin, wavering, and the colors shadowed, to give the impression of the dream he was trying to capture, now he wanted strong lines and primary colors. "Clean and simple," he muttered. When the canvas was completely white, he went to the window and gazed at the peak.

Maneuvering the Hope around two consecutive, nearly three-hundred-sixty-degree turns, Joy thought the scene looked like a bad postcard. The photographer had managed depth poorly; the mountains seemed two-dimensional. The face of the peak looked like a blunted arrowhead.

Hallelujah Hole left no doubt that it was a broken-down town. For Sale signs outnumbered traffic signs. Even the possibility of rebirth as a ski area was denied by the piles of tailings which disfigured every nearby slope. There was no supermarket. Before going on to another town, Joy decided to claim dishes and utensils from Max and so save him a trip up to the cabin.

"Well, little one, you're up and at it early this morning. I was just doing up a package for you people."

Four brown plastic dishes, flatware from a defunct restaurant, two iron frying pans, and a wire whisk made up Max's version of a starter set.

"Salt and pepper?" she suggested. "A casserole? Mixing bowl, carving knife . . ." Eyes closed, she enumerated. Max obliged as far as he was able. His produce did not appeal to her. There was mold on the squash. She made a token purchase of a quart of milk. He carried the box of things to the car, told her to drive carefully, and pinched her cheek. Apparently he had decided fatherly flirtatiousness best suited their relationship.

Love in a Cabin

"These mountain roads are a bitch until you get used to 'em."

Several miles down the road the town of Silver Plume boasted a hot spring and thus a built-in prosperity. Unlike the gold ore in the area, the hot water kept coming and so did patients and tourists. There were two supermarkets, a hotel in the grand manner, railroad tracks. Joy purchased what they needed and then settled down at a lunch counter with a cup of coffee to write a postcard.

Dearest Father, We have arrived and I am well . . .

She paused; invention faltered. What in the world more could she say to him? But the brevity looked a bit unloving.

The weather is splendid.

She scrawled it very large to cover the rest of the card. Thinking of him at his desk parsing "the lineaments of gratified desire" or some other puzzling passage, she laughed affectionately and addressed the card.

Outside she hesitated before a mailbox as it occurred to her for the first time that they were without an address. No one knew where they were. It was the most exciting thing in the world: they were a unit, they were alone.

Of course, they were not really alone. Max kept a daily eye on them under the guise of amending the cabin. Day after day he brought gifts: a rubber plant, plums rubbed to a sheen with vegetable oil, a large calendar from a masonry supply company bearing an illustration of the Old West entitled *Laugh Kills Lonesome*—and more. The liberality of his devotion amazed them.

"He's in love with you," Stephen teased. "It's like the

twelve days of Christmas around here. Today the French hens, tomorrow the calling birds."

"English hens, not French hens," she said, examining the Rock Cornish hens which Max said he got free from a wholesaler. "A bread stuffing and an orange glaze will suit just beautifully."

"Go to it, girl, with zeal." He went back to his painting, pleased to have her occupied.

Later, while devouring the hens, they agreed that the trouble with Max was he couldn't be stopped. Tactics were necessary in the absence of barricades, some kind of pact; for Max had a dreadnought curiosity about painting and how it got done. He would make his day's offering, then move from Joy's kitchen to Stephen's studio and ask, in a voice deepened by the seriousness of the subject, "How's it going?"

"OK," Stephen would reply in a tone less strenuously appropriate.

Apprised of the fact that Stephen was painting the scene from the studio window, Max obviously expected a mountain—pleasantly familiar, if not wholly exact—to come to the canvas—soon.

Finally exasperated, Stephen shouted one morning, "Look, Max—there!" He grabbed the hook and pulled him to a window, thinking how strange it was that one did things with a man's hook that one wouldn't do with a man's hand. "Look. What do you see?"

"Mountain."

"But when it gets to your eyes, what's it really made of?"

"Rock." Mouth all set to laugh, Max was a portrait of

a man who knows when he's being had. When Stephen didn't spring the joke, Max strained his eyes and tried again. "Stone?"

Stephen muttered something about planes of light and gave up. Instead he gently explained that he could only do his work when the light was right and it would be fine if Max would talk to Joy whenever he felt like a ride up to the cabin, because Joy absolutely loved his company and the chance for a chat, but it would be a favor most appreciated if he, Max, would leave him, Stephen, alone to paint in the prime of the day.

Max did not really understand, but he did comply. His gifts ceased, but his affection continued. He often came to see Joy. During the first week of his visits under the new rule of the house, she commiserated with a gashed foot requiring three stitches, an allergic reaction to a bee sting, and a bent fender.

Stephen worked all the time. He still ate but he didn't always sleep. Joy cooked and devoted herself to the long-ledger. The days became routine. Soon they were even accustomed to the smell of propane gas.

After ten days, a large area of Stephen's canvas was still white, but he had done innumerable quick sketches and color studies of the peak at all times of the day and in different kinds of weather. At the base of the peak's face the crest of a glacier was just visible. Its coloration was the thing giving him the most trouble. He had begun a collection of facts and legends about the peak; also begun was Joy's fear of the peak and what it was coming to mean to him.

One night after dinner he tried to explain. He said the

peak lured people, changed people, sometimes killed them, but although it was often violent and strange, it was also simple, beautiful, and natural. The peak contained all things in harmony and so it was important to paint it. He explained that to paint was to bring things to order, to make them sit down in one place. It was very difficult because there was so much disorder around. Storm and death were part of the peak—but not disorder.

Joy said she did not understand how he got all that meaning out of a mountain. The peak looked like such a barren place. She went to work on the long-ledger. Stephen read a pamphlet history of the area.

"Do you know that nobody was able to mount the face until 1960?"

"What do you mean by 'mount' it?" She did not look up from the long-ledger.

"Climb it, accomplish it, get to the top."

"Oh, damn the mountain."

He examined the angle of her bowed head. They were on their way to trouble about something. It was necessary to ease things out. Life in a cabin was too frugal for her, too dull, or perhaps she was about to get her period.

"Tell you what, match girl . . ." he flung himself down on the floor by her chair and put his arms around her legs, "Let's go for a picnic tomorrow—a lavish one, someplace beautiful where we can swim. Would you like that?"

"Yes. I'm bored out of my mind with this, really I am." She tossed the long-ledger onto the coffee table.

The next morning they hiked into a wilderness recommended by Max for its solitude. "Nothing there but the marmots," he promised. He was wrong. Although they met no one, litter was everywhere: the usual cans and wrappers and occasionally something more sordid—a discarded tampon or condom.

They carried tuna sandwiches carefully garnished, beer donated by Max, Joy's lady poet, and Stephen's paints. He would not be persuaded to leave them at home. The midmorning sun was intense.

"I am legs walking, skin burning—nothing more," said Joy. It was a good feeling.

"Someone once talked about the kind of sun which burns out every question—I can't remember who. This is what he meant."

"Just walk, don't think, Stephen."

They kept a steady rhythm for four miles until they reached Diana's Lake. The clear mountain water was inviting.

"A chaste but pagan grotto," Stephen proclaimed, setting up his easel. "I will paint you light. Garish and gaudy, in very bad taste. Light for Joy, wherever she is. Compact, portable, easily placed on any wall . . . the light of this morning."

He worked while she tried once again to get on with the lady poet and, failing that, collected pieces of shiny black obsidian and fool's gold.

In less than an hour he came to find her, apologetic for his neglect of her.

"Come see. It's for you, as I promised."

She was astounded. It was the best thing of his she'd ever seen. The dryness of the air, the scorch of the sun, the cold clarity of the water were there on canvas to be felt.

"I can't tell you, Stephen . . . how beautiful . . ."

He took her in his arms; unspoken but painful between them was the fact that she was not often so wholehearted about his work.

The place remained deserted. In the early afternoon they tried to swim nude in the lake but the water was far too cold. Instead they sat naked on the bank, ankled in ice, fire on their backs, enjoying sandwiches and beer.

Cousin Patricia—something of a stranger lately— flicked in, flicked out. She was fully clothed and also protected by wide-brimmed straw. "Adam and Eve," she sneered.

As if he too were haunted by her, Stephen picked up the theme, whispering, "Sometimes I look at a canvas and I say to myself, I'll paint Joy, but I never do paint you, because as soon as I get you clearly in focus, I'm too distracted to paint . . . ah, where to begin . . . I leer gluttonously and then bite in. The apple's plucked again."

"I thought you'd given up rhyme."

"You provoke a lyric mood," he said, running his hand along her thigh, "a strange hilarity."

Suddenly he turned away from her and pointed. "Joy, look . . . Up there . . . Hello, up there! Who are you? The angel who guards or the dirty old man who watches? Declare yourself. Shout down to us, come on. Wave to him, Joy."

On the ledge of rock above them: a shadow, a hulk, a

man looking down impassively. He did not return their salutations. By the time they dressed he was gone.

Coming down the mountain, they took a route which led them within sight of Selma's stone cabin. They had not seen her since the night of their arrival and Max was oddly silent about her. The path leading to her cabin was blocked by an erection of large stones—a signal, a cairn, or a totem; they could not guess its meaning. Impelled by curiosity as well as courtesy, Joy decided to pay her promised call upon Selma the next day.

The next morning the stones no longer guarded the path. Joy noticed evidence of recent digging along its edges; some kind of cultivation was going on. She approached the cabin cautiously, unsure of Mr. Quick's reaction to visits from near strangers.

It was an unusual little house and an old one. The stone was well weathered. The slit-like recessed windows reminded her of those in medieval churches designed so that lepers could look on remotely as the glories of God were celebrated. It was the sort of place that bore mute testimony to an interesting, if not sacred, past, but now from its roof there rose, eloquent as a spire, the tallest TV antenna Joy had ever seen. It was directional, it was UHF.

There was no answer to her knock, but Mr. Quick appeared around the corner of the house, stretched out his forelegs and arched his rump, as if bowing, and led her to the back of the house. There was Selma, in a doorless outhouse, her Wranglers around her ankles, a can of

Coors in one hand and red leatherbound book in the other.

"This guy says, 'It isn't life that matters but the strength with which you live it.' Crap, I say. Crap." Selma was graphic. "It's life that matters." Apparently she was a critic as well as purveyor of aphorisms. "Well, I didn't know you were coming, so I won't apologize . . ." She hiked up her pants. "Because if there's one thing I can't stand, it's a minuet."

"Thank God we've got plumbing," was all Joy could manage.

"Oh, I got plumbing all right, it isn't that." Selma led the way into the house. "It went on the blink and I didn't feel like having Max up to fix it. No, I just wanted to be alone for awhile. When I put up some stones down there on the path, Max understands. Sit yourself down. Beer?"

"No, thanks."

"Not in the morning, huh. Well, I like it all the time. Coffee?"

"Please don't go to any trouble. I just came up to say hello."

"What did I just say about minuets? Now, do you or don't you want some coffee."

"I'd love some."

"Good." Selma went into the kitchen.

For the first time Joy noticed that the TV was on. The test pattern of the educational network glowed in a corner of the small dark room. There was a pile of *Time* magazines on the floor, the top one bearing a portrait of the assassinated politician. She picked it up.

Love in a Cabin

"Awful, wasn't it?" Selma handed her a mug of coffee. "That's what did it to me this time. Every once in awhile —whump. The trap door opens and down I go, down to the blue devils. I was OK for a few days after it happened, but then—whump."

"I know. A funk. I used to have them all the time before Stephen."

"Yes, love helps." Mr. Quick snorkled up Selma's leg and into her lap. "I was married once." She mooned at the test pattern, as if contemplating breakfast for two and coupling at twilight.

"What happened?" Joy asked in a flat-footed way, determined not to be found guilty of a minuet.

"All the good things got thrown out with the garbage that goes on between people." Selma pushed Mr. Quick's head away and went to collect another Coors.

Joy scrutinized a bookshelf. There was a line of books all bound in the same way as the one Selma was reading and all by an author with a penchant for one-syllable virtues and sins as titles.

Selma shambled back again, popping a metal ring. "I've been through *Truth, Greed,* and *Pride* and let me tell you, the guy's half-assed."

"Oversimplifies, does he?"

"You can bet your bottom dollar he does, sweetie. There's no noon when everyone sings up to God, and there's no one night when you sell your soul. You make transactions instead. All kinds of transactions. And arrangements."

Delivered of wisdom, she sank to the floor, rested her chin on her knees, sipped, stared at the cover of *Time*.

Her greying blond hair strayed over her eyes. She tried to clear the catarrh from her voice. "Life is seepage."

Joy put a firm hand on a trembling bone. "Are you all right?" It was a very general question.

"Most of the time—sure." The voice was gaining control; the bones picked themselves up off the floor—surprisingly agile, almost graceful. "It's just that sometimes I go off . . . I get derailed like an old train. I get screaming mad at things. Whump."

"Well, now . . ." Joy wanted to shake the conversation up, slap it on the wrists, get the circulation moving, but she didn't quite know how. "What a handsome boy." She pointed to a photograph on the bookshelf. A young face smiled out from a uniform.

"That's my kid." Selma picked up the photograph and examined it, as if expecting to find something new in it since the last time she looked. "Military school. I hope to hell they're socking some sense into him. I don't see him much. My ex has had him for years. Like I was saying—transactions, arrangements. What about you? Tell me about yourself. You're from back east, right?"

"Yes. There's not much to tell really. My mother's dead, my father's a teacher. I used to have a job, but now my life is Stephen."

"Is he good to you?" The question had a carnal ring.

"Yes, very good."

"Max is good to me. You might not believe it of old Max, but he is."

"Do you stay here through the winter?"

"Haven't you seen the gates up the road? They close the mountains off in stages as the snow comes. Max stays down in the town, of course, but I go on. Usually to the coast. Quick and me, we like the coast—don't we, boy, don't we, lover?" She slapped his flanks.

Suddenly the tube came alive: NET was broadcasting.

"I like to keep in touch," Selma said.

Anthropology in a leather-patched jacket explained that only a cosmic age ago, the species was amphibious.

"So what else is new," heckled Selma.

The march of dead soldiers continued, can after can. A Chinese chef scaled and caressed a carp before red boiling. An angular creature with a British accent was informative on the subject of the potted geranium. "The geranium isn't the only potted thing. Whew." Selma was at least candid about her condition.

Later, they walked down to the road. Cultivation *was* going on. Selma was transplanting wildflowers from the reclamation project to the edge of her path: blackeyed Susans, buttercups, Queen Anne's Lace. Rarity of species was not the point.

The giant Caterpillar slugged back and forth.

"What are they doing?"

"I don't know, they don't know. You'd think reclamation would mean putting things back the way they were. That isn't what it means. It makes me mad."

Joy quickly changed the subject. Together they transferred harebells, while Selma, considerably sobered by air and work, discoursed upon the corruption of dog racing—stones embedded in a paw to slow a dog down, water before a race to make a dog pee instead of run. She patted Mr. Quick for the wrongs of his past. "It makes me mad."

They parted late in the afternoon. Joy extended an in-

vitation to dinner—it was meatloaf, there was more than
enough—but Selma said she wasn't eating much these
days. Some other time. She seemed almost gay.

"Besotted," said Patricia, appearing among the trees.
"A lush."

There was more to Selma than that, Joy thought.
Selma risked herself; she suffered, so one didn't mind
her banality. Her aphorisms were trophies earned; there
was much truth in what she said.

At the cabin, Stephen and the Hope were gone. Joy
sat down with the long-ledger to wait.

Life is seepage, she wrote, and then proceeded to a description of her day with Selma. In the middle of a cata-
logue of wildflowers she stopped. It was getting so that
when something happened she thought first, Oh, I
must get this down, before I lose it, before I forget it—
only secondly did she think about what was actually happening. There was poor Selma, served up cold and flat
on the page. As a penance she gave up the long-ledger
and started the meatloaf. When Stephen came in, she
licked tomato sauce from her fingers and involved him
in a bear hug.

"Looks good. Am I having you or what's in the bowl?"

"You're having meatloaf. I can hardly wait. I feed, I
feed, like a pig at a trough I feed. Flesh slops over the
bone."

"It's not quite that bad, darling. In fact, it's rather
nice. Sort of Renaissance." He patted her buttocks.

"Renaissance went out with the Renaissance. I think
Selma's starving."

"I've spent the whole damn day with Max—not a

stroke of work done." He looked longingly in the direction of the studio. "His house slipped again. It tilts at
about the same angle the earth tilts. He came up this
morning just after you left and said he needed an extra
hand—if you'll excuse the expression—and I didn't know
how to say no to him. We did some shoring up with a
'53 Chevy, but it's not going to last. While we were doing that, he told me something about Selma. She goes
a little mad once in awhile. Hair streaming, clothes fly-
ing, she roars and rages all over the mountain like a
banshee on the stormy moor. Max seems to think it's
tied up with the moon."

"Oh, nonsense. She gets depressed and likes to walk
and be alone. She's just coming out of a seige." Joy put
the meat in the oven and scowled at the clock. "Dinner
in an hour. I think she just drinks beer all day and doesn't
eat. She's lost weight since we first saw her."

To her dismay, Stephen shrugged and headed for the
studio. She wanted to talk to him about Selma. He was
back in a matter of minutes. "The good light's gone; I
can't concentrate; what's the point." He prowled around
the kitchen.

"Stephen, she is nothing but bones."

"Maybe she's got the right idea. Maybe we should all
go starving mad now and again—just to see what it's
like."

She put down a carrot and paring knife and squared
off in the middle of his pacing path. "Exactly what's got
into you tonight?"

"I don't know. Tonight I'd like to blow some grass or
drop some acid. I feel . . . out of touch."

"Out of touch with what?"

He turned his back on her and looked out the window.

"With red foxes baying at a white moon. With a country I can't even remember except when I'm dreaming. With possibility. I'd like to fly up there . . ." he pointed to the peak, "and have a talk out with the Prime Cause. Selma haunting around the mountain at midnight—I'll bet she's in touch."

"To the contrary. Selma believes keeping in touch has something to do with TV and *Time* magazine, and she makes a great deal more sense than you do."

"You are such a hausfrau." He stamped back to the studio.

Her stomach took an elevator ride down. He so rarely spoke of his experiments with drugs. Most of the time it was as if he'd lopped those months off his life—a clean amputation. Now this. For reassurance she looked to the painting of Diana's Lake—her painting—which hung on the back of the kitchen door; then she turned to the gravy. It needed clarification. Moments later he was back again. He came up behind her, turned her around, waltzed her up and down, and rhymed to make her laugh:

"We have our own countree, a country apart, a country of heart." Then, more seriously: "This is the country to which I truly belong." He kissed her gently and made her look at him. "What do you see?"

"All the joy in the world."

"No, Joy, no. That's too much for one person to be."

The meatloaf was adequate, the conversation cheerful,

and he helped with the dishes. When he went back to work, pleased to have things straight again, it was with renewed purpose. If there was no real light, then he'd work by electric light. The whole night was ahead of him; no people would get in the way.

It went like a streak. He was burning with it, he was boiling with it—wham, out it came. A painting was done! He was in awe of himself. But that wasn't all, there was more left over. He began to rough out sketches for a larger painting of the peak and the surrounding mountains.

I'm white heat, I'm dry ice, he thought, believing it and, at the same time, laughing at himself for believing it.

When Max's knock came—steel on wood with a hollow tap, tap—he held his breath. No more houses, no more cars, no more jinx—not tonight. Joy's voice from the other room was a placating hum. He heard the leg of the coffee table scratch the floor: Max was sitting down on the couch. Stephen relaxed. They would talk about Selma and leave him alone.

When Max finally left, Joy knocked on the studio door. Stephen did not invite her in to look at the finished painting. His excitement with it was still vivid, and he didn't wish to risk a damper. Standing in the doorway, he kissed her good-night and said: "I'll stay up for awhile, I think."

He continued to sketch, dimly aware of the sounds of her bedding down: the shower, the closet door, the bedsprings. Sometime after midnight he felt himself go off the boil. He knew if he went on sketching it would all be bad, and if he looked at the completed painting perhaps he would think it was not so good as he first supposed. Instead he took a walk.

Mercury, Venus, and Mars were out of view, and Saturn had not yet risen. In the pale light of the new moon, the peak seemed less spectacular than usual; it was hardly to be distinguished from the more ordinary mountains around it. The macabre shadows of the trees overhanging the road were, for the moment, more interesting. When he got back to the cabin, he knew he wouldn't be able to sleep. Too many gears were still meshing. He settled down on the couch with one of his histories of the region. Browsing idly through flora, fauna, and anecdote, he was suddenly struck by an old photograph of a stone cottage. It was the one Selma was renting from Max. Its previous inhabitants were legendary: a retired prospector reputed to have left deeds, and perhaps even gold itself, in the walls; a renegade monk who carved more than three thousand crucifixes from native wood, then burnt them all in a clearing one moonless night; a hermit ornithologist who recorded not the calls but the language of birds—a complete grammar and lexicon. Apparently Selma was a legitimate heiress to the place.

He went into the bedroom to read the passage to Joy, but she was asleep. She lay curled, one hand gripping a knee, the other a shoulder. Her mouth was moving. She seemed to be making a speech. Something was worrying her.

The long dining room table was set formally for six and

the crystal predicted two kinds of wine. Candles cast a dubious light. The hostess was there but Joy couldn't make out who it was—Selma or Cousin Patricia or perhaps her dead mother. "What do you want from me?" she was asking. "What is it you want?"

Cabin Fever

"Do you think it's masculine or feminine?"

"Neither. It's nothing, it's neuter, it's dead."

"Oh, moan, poor Joy's jealous of stone."

Joy looked around the studio with disgust. Turpentine-soaked rags and crumpled sketches were scattered over every surface. He was working on two paintings at once; there wasn't space to move in the room. Although he occasionally catnapped on the couch, he hadn't really been to bed in weeks. He hardly spoke to her and when he did, it was almost always in rhyme. Running out of canvas one day, he painted on a wall. Who did he think he was, Gauguin? When Max found out, he was going to be furious. Max was already angry. "He don't take care of you right, little one. He oughtta know better," Max said. It was all she could do to keep him from saying something to Stephen and making matters worse.

For some reason Stephen couldn't make love. She missed him.

Finished paintings of all sizes leaned from floor to wall around the room—noisy, gashed with color. Endlessly the peak: the peak from this position, the peak from that position, the peak with every possible thing going on around it. He was the peak's pornographer.

"Princess, Snow White, Cinderella, poor little match girl, why so sad?" He pulled his face into an imitation of her frown.

"Stephen, we've got to do something."

"I know, I know. I'm not the prince. I'm the real, unadorned, clammy frog. You still like my clammy mouth, don't you, little match girl, and my froggy hands? Like this . . ."

Her response to his hands was immediate and powerful.

"Please don't, Stephen."

"You used to say my hands were magical and knew everything. You used to like my hands, Joy."

"I still do, far too much. That's why you mustn't do this to me. It isn't fair to me."

"It will be good this time. I know it will be good. This time it will be right."

"No, Stephen, please . . . It isn't going to be right this time and I can't go through it again. Please . . . you must stop." She pushed him away.

"A splint, a splint of log for the rubbery frog who can't get it up anymore."

"Something must be done. We can't go on this way."

"What did you say?"

"That we can't go on this way."

"Hear Joy say we can't go on this way. Joy's talking like a play. Are we in a play, Joy? What kind of a play are we in?"

"Stephen, please . . ."

"Yes, quite right, something must be done; send out proclamations and make preparations! Kiss the frog, and then in the last-act nick of time—enter the prince. The prince always does something. That's what he's for. Come on, Joy, kiss the frog."

She did and suddenly he came down from the stage and seemed quite normal. "Don't worry, I'm all right. Just let me finish off these . . ." he gestured toward the two paintings, one on an easel, the other propped against the back of a chair.

Joy went back to the long-ledger, described the motions of a fly as it negotiated the horizon of a ripening tomato on the kitchen sill, and then slammed the book shut. Although not as good as screaming, walking was certainly better than flies. She went up to see Selma.

"Stupid bastard." Selma was just annihilating a late night talker with a turn of the knob. "Well, sweetie, what's new in paradise these days?"

"Snakes."

Stephen finished the two paintings and started two more. Joy cooked and explored the surrounding mountains in the Rueful Hope. As the summer reached its zenith, she watched ghost towns become boom towns, invaded by fluid colonies of young people who vied with rot and rats for a summer's possession. Sometimes Joy spoke with them. They were generous, well-meaning people, but they were also sad people. Their conversation was seasoned with the phrase "you know," suggesting a rapport which did not exist. Joy didn't know. She recorded what they said in the long-ledger, but she still couldn't make out what it was they were really after.

By the middle of August the countryside was up in arms. Selectmen held emergency sessions about sanitation. Max was vehement on the subject: "Filth, that's what they are." He clenched his fist and shook it. "That's the only language they understand." Injunctions were issued. The young people departed.

Joy found herself more in tune with a sixteen-year-old runaway who worked at the livery stable in Hallelujah Hole and called himself Iowa Jim. They talked about the problem of God and agreed that they did not believe in any Manichaean duality; they liked to think that God was all around them. Jim said he prayed the war would end before he was made to go to it. He wasn't quite sure he could handle war. He wasn't yellow or anything like that—Joy wasn't to get the wrong idea—but he didn't even like hunting, for Chrissake. Sometimes Jim lent her a slow, amiable, overweight gelding and they rode up easy trails.

One day, presumably suffering from an excess of theology, Jim grabbed her and kissed her. She liked it far too much and decided discretion was perhaps the better part of self-control. She did not return to the livery stable.

One or two evenings a week she went up to watch the news with Selma. Sometimes Stephen accompanied her. Often Max was there.

Through July, through August, Biafra went on starving. CARE couldn't reach, so they didn't contribute.

"Maybe we should send a check . . ."

"Maybe we should . . ."

"But if they can't get the food through . . ."

Czechoslovakia was in trouble and they pitied her, because it was for the second time.

"That's where it all started," said Max, brandishing his hook ambiguously.

The impending election confused them. Max said he'd probably go Republican like always—because of the hand. His logic escaped them, but they refrained from saying so. Selma said she didn't know what to think; it just made her so damn mad.

Stephen, who usually managed to stay lucid and non-rhyming through the news, shrewdly observed that THEIR candidate said everything in double and triple negatives. His every second word was a form of no. "I don't really want to run, but I can't not run," Stephen mimicked in the voice of a man just getting over a head cold. "I don't see how we can not let youth be heard."

They watched films of extended arms and chanting voices. "So what's the difference between 'Peace!' and 'Heil!', anyway," grumbled Selma. She said she understood how they felt, but she didn't like the way they did things.

"I tell you, what's going on out there," Max pointed at the set as if "out there" were somehow housed in it, "isn't a gap, it's a war." He stared with suspicion at Stephen, who was grizzled and hollow-eyed from working. Clearly Max thought he was making some enormous connection between vital matters.

Early in September they gathered at Selma's cabin for the opening night violence at the Chicago nominating convention. They watched the army advance upon the young people, watched blows, watched blood. Stephen paced back and forth behind their chairs. "We should be there," he said to Joy.

Max turned around, looked at Stephen, and said, "Yeah, kid, maybe you should be there." His voice was like a bayonet.

"Transactions," said Selma out of the blue. "We all make transactions, Stevie."

He nodded. "I guess I'll be going."

Joy rose to go with him. He pressed her shoulder. "Stay. I'll work for awhile."

Selma walked him to the door and partway down the path.

"Don't mind Max. He means well."

"I understand that."

She offered him her beer. "Loving cup."

He smiled in the dark and sipped.

"You all right, Stevie?"

"Sure. How about yourself?"

She scuffed her foot back and forth. "I'll keep myself together one way or another."

"You do that. For me." He took her in his arms and kissed her, trying to muster and focus all his passion in order to protect her for that one moment. She was trembling when he released her. They stood a little apart, arms resting on each other's shoulders. He saw that she wanted to speak but could think of nothing appropriate. To save her the awkwardness, he turned away and headed down the path, straining his eyes for a glimpse of Mercury lying very low in the west.

At the cabin he heated coffee and drank a large cup.

"Time, time, time," chanted his chorale.

The nightmare was back whenever he slept, and as before he couldn't recall it when he awoke—only his fear of it. He slept as little as possible.

He was working on a cycle of storms: rain, lightning, hail, snow. The peak created every kind of weather, while down where they were, weather was unusually static and predictable. Day after day, the sun sat squarely overhead until half-past three, and then it rained for fifteen minutes. At sunset there was no breath of wind for one hour—the dead hour, Joy called it. It made her uneasy, she said—all that silence and nothing moving. He walked around the studio, picking up a painting here and there, reviewing his work.

He did not know what earthly good could be expected from paintings of a mountain or why they were so important to him.

It was natural to go up and down about his work. Tonight he was down. He told himself not to worry. He needed to get away from the smell of turpentine. He needed air. Tomorrow he'd take a hike, stretch himself, not think, not work.

Joy and Selma planned a trip to Silver Plume for the next morning. A number of birds were going to be killed with one stone: the laundromat, the beauty parlor, shopping, and whatever else caught their fancy. "Here's to freewheeling," crowed Selma. "We'll spend some change."

Max walked Joy down to the cabin, surveyed the Rueful Hope disparagingly, and kicked its tires. "You be careful, little one," he cautioned, pecking her on the cheek. He watched her open the cabin door as if he were afraid she might, just might, be walking into the jaws of hell.

Stephen was in the bathroom peering at himself in the small rectangle of cracked mirror above the basin. Joy came up behind him.

"That man you see isn't me." The opinion was delivered from a reflection to a reflection. "That's the anti-Stephen in the anti-cosmos."

"God," said Joy.

Cousin Patricia materialized in the mirror—a third reflection. "Tsk, tsk, tsk, *dégringolade* of a Child of the Times," she said.

"This man's got to get himself born again." Stephen surveyed his week's growth and lathered briskly.

High Life

"I think Selma's girdled. She's mincing," Stephen declared from the window.

Joy joined him to watch the phenomenon arrive.

Selma came down the path in a dress, carrying a small laundry bag. Trousered for so long on the mountain, she walked uneasily, as if the least extravagance of motion might lead to humiliation and perhaps disgrace.

"How dreadful," Joy said. Selma was starving to death; now she was sure of it. Her dress festooned her bones. It was two sizes too large at least. Even her open-toed, straw shoes were now a bad fit.

Cheeks, lips, and fingernails were shakily reddened. The effort was stupendous; they could only applaud. She presented herself to them in a fret of uncertainty. Her gestures were spastic.

"I got nothing to wear, nothing fits. How can I go

like this? I look like something that belongs in a cage."

Joy mentally crossed fingers and offered prayers for a steady, honest voice. "Don't be silly, Selma, you look just fine."

"Now, Stevie, tell me the truth."

"Selma, you're beautiful."

"Oh, go on . . ."

"You go on . . ." He steered her out to the Rueful Hope and opened the door for her gallantly. Then he turned to Joy and took her hands in his.

"See you later," he said.

"Yes." She pressed his hands and released them.

Joy and Selma stopped in Hallelujah Hole just long enough to give Max a honk on the horn. He came to the door of the store, and his whistle was something left over from V-E Day.

Stephen laced up combat boots illegally conveyed from the promised land. They were perfect for hiking. He stamped his foot to test the tautness of the lacing. In such dry weather, acclimatized as he was to the altitude, he was good for fifteen miles, in spite of lack of sleep. The fifteen miles were owed him after weeks—no, months of work.

He spread the mouth of his small backpack and put into it a canteen of water from their stream, two sandwiches made from leftovers in the refrigerator, a survey map of the area, and as a last thought a three-by-five sketch book and an HB pencil. He combed the cabin for his compass and finally found it in the depths of a drawer, wrapped in one of his socks. Apparently Joy thought the directional god evaporated from a compass if it were left to sit airing in plain sight.

Before leaving, he looked once more around the cabin, spied and retrieved the long-ledger from under the coffee table. When not attached to it like a drowner to a life-line, Joy strewed those leaves of her life about with care-less indifference. He was forever finding it under foot, picking it up, and putting it someplace obvious so she wouldn't suddenly ram around the place looking for it like a virago in unexpected heat. He placed the book on the kitchen table, very gently, just in case Joy herself might somehow persist in it. The patina of civilization was very thin, and below that surface he was a caveman with a healthy respect for mana. He gave the long-ledger an extra pat for luck.

The morning was already losing its early coolness. He strode down the road, pacing himself, setting a deliber-ate breathing rhythm. Mr. Quick appeared and trailed him diffidently.

"Come on, Quick, it's all right. Heel."

Selma and Joy decided to get the worst over first. They chose the launderette in Silver Plume's largest shopping center because it had an extractor. "Lord knows, we don't want to spend all day waiting for the towels to dry," Selma said.

She jammed coins into the washing machine as if she expected a jackpot. "The problem with love is that it just plain wears you out."

"You are so right." Getting an amber light, Joy added bleach. "He never sleeps, and I lie awake worrying about him, listening for him, trying to guess what he's doing, what he's thinking, from the noises in the studio. It just can't go on, but as soon as I make up my mind to do something about it, of course he seems better. For example, this morning he was very much himself. I don't know, I just don't know." She gazed hypnotically through the porthole at the churning white water.

"Don't you worry now. As soon as we're done here, we're going to go buy you some razzle-dazzle, something really . . ." Selma sketched voluptuousness in the air. "That'll take his mind off his pictures."

"Nothing is ever going to take his mind off his work, I'm afraid. I just have to make up my mind if I want to go on living with it."

"I always say, don't go looking for earthquakes; they'll find you."

At the foot of the first ascent, Stephen stopped briefly to rest. Sitting on a stone fence, he admired two very old white horses in a pasture. Nose to tail, tail to nose, they flicked flies from one another.

"Social security and the compensations of the hearth," he explained to Mr. Quick, who barked empathetically at the horses.

Riding a sleek black mare, Joy's friend Iowa Jim came down the road, heroic in faded, skintight jeans belted with silver that caught and played with the sun. He gave Stephen the two-fingered V. Stephen returned it and began to climb.

The road to the ranger station was steep. Halfway there the dog gave up and turned back.

There was no escaping the fact that Selma attracted attention. She was too much the human condition—in a mess. People with eyes for eccentricity stared; having seen, they turned strictly away and pretended to be busy doing something else.

"Walk," flashed the sign. Joy took Selma's arm protectively.

Stephen opened the door of the cubicle and read the logbook for the day. A party of six with a guide had mounted the face of the peak by the most hazardous route at two in the morning. Stephen remembered that the peak's weather was considered most dangerous during the day, not at night as one might expect. It was a slow day on the mountain. He signed his name, noted the time—10:30 A. M.—and put a question mark under the category *Destination*. He wouldn't know that until he checked his map. He hoped there was a fairly easy trail to the base of the peak. A weather report was tacked above the logbook:

> High winds. Wind-chilled temps.
> of 20 degrees during the day.
> Subzero temps. at night.
> COLD SNOW WIND ICE COLD SNOW

The report pertained to the summit, two thousand feet above the place he planned to reach. A crudely carved slab of wood directed him: *TO TRAIL HEADS.*

He swung down the path in an easy stride. It was good to walk, but better to work. The darting flight of a Clark's nutcracker, the aspen on the razor-edge of turning —all, all was getting away from him. The sketch pad burnt into his back. But he promised himself—not for another half hour. He'd just work his body for a half hour. Exercise was important. Also sleep . . . he didn't do enough of that either. Conservation of energy was the name of the law he'd broken. Between the legs he was dead and without thinking about it, without wanting to, he rhymed all the time. He resolved to dismiss the voices that nagged "No time, no time." He resolved to spend more time with Joy. What a bad, unfair time he gave her. Yet he still believed that if they could just keep what they had intact . . .

It was necessary to take care; if he wasn't careful, he'd never harvest himself.

The gay phosphorescent dusk was like a corridor for terminal patients. Selma was having the works: wash, cut, color rinse, and set. Joy settled for just a wash because Stephen liked her hair long and unornamented with curl. Under the dryer, not reading the copy of *Ladies' Home Journal* on her lap, Joy watched the white-gowned, platinum beautician operate upon Selma, who with a groan of real pain just managed to survive the shock therapy of a three-way mirror in the booth. Extended in the complicated chair like a huge doll with a broken neck, Selma submitted to water too hot, water too cold, and a crown of shampoo. The stations of suffering passed across her face in a series of grimaces. Joy forced her attention upon a recipe for stuffed mackerel in *Ladies' Home Journal*.

Stephen chose a six-mile trail with a thirty-percent grade. According to the map, it led to Iceberg Tarn at the base of the peak and would afford a fine view of the glacier. He dug the sketch pad and pencil out of his pack, cursing himself for a fool. It was the colors he wanted; it would have made more sense to bring his pastels. He released the compass needle, tapped the case, and headed west. His skin first registered the slight darkening of the sky; then he looked up. A grey filter seemed to be passing across the sun. It was just as well it was cooling off.

The bells of noon clanged in Silver Plume. In Penney's they discovered a sale. Coiffed within an inch of her life, in a color that was slightly to the right of lemon, Selma browsed through the fall collection while Joy tried on late summer reductions and finally presented herself for inspection in a low-cut sundress that fit like a dream.

"Oh, la!" Selma was aghast with admiration.

Stephen sat on a tree stump, sketched the profusion of snow buttercups, sibbaldia, and Indian paintbrush at his feet, ate half a sandwich, and began again to climb.

The trail was narrower now and steeper. Occasionally, from a great distance, an explosive thud reported that some hunting season or other was in progress. The aspen were shrunken, more twisted, shorter-lived; their grey corpses littered his path. He noticed evidence of what appeared to be someone hiking ahead of him: cigarettes freshly field-stripped, jays scolding as though recently disturbed, crowds of alarmed grasshoppers clicking and jumping. However, he saw no one, and no one was logged out for the trail he was on.

Breathless suddenly, he was forced to recognize the altitude with respect and rest again. An overturned tree trunk nearby intrigued him; it looked like an enormous starfish gaping for air. He sketched and argued with himself about his work.

And if it had nothing to do with anything . . . with Ali Baba and the hills of Jerusalem, with murder and invasion? What if . . . unconnected . . . Well, then . . .

He did not finish the thought but climbed once more in the sea-grey light. One horsefly clung to him like a pilot fish. He was close to the timberline.

It was ladies' day at the rodeo. Women were allowed in at half price. It was the last performance of the season, and the place was packed. The gate was dedicated to the Disabled Veterans, and a wheelchair brigade of them began the show, circling the arena once while a scratched recording of "America the Beautiful" played over the PA. Then came the parade of performers on horseback led by the World Champion All Around Cowboy and the Girl Champion Barrel Racer, prancing and whooping their hats.

"You'll be seeing the nation's top R.C.A. rodeo cowboys in action, against some of the meanest, wiliest, manhatin' brutes the livestock contractor could round up, so give a big hand to every game try, whether it's win or lose."

In the interim between announcement and first event, while clowns cavorted on a fire engine, Selma signaled a vendor for beer and explained the effect bad draws could have on a bareback bronc rider's licking and timing. Although she much preferred the dogs, Selma knew a thing or two about rodeos. Her dissertation upon the intricacies of scoring was just begun when a chute opened and the first horse and rider erupted.

Calf roping, steer wrestling, and bull riding followed. Joy rooted for the calves, steer, hump-backed Brahmas, and the buffalo Gregory, trained to walk on his knees, who appeared during intermission. Throughout the afternoon Selma was hard put to explain to Joy that she was missing the point and also what the point exactly was.

"Sweetie, you're supposed to cheer for the man not the animal."

"Why on earth do that? The man's in it because he wants to be. The animal doesn't have a choice."

Selma groaned and replied that a rodeo was no place for a bleeding heart.

Stephen accomplished a steep pitch and found himself on the ridge of a col. All trees, all shrubs, all colors but shades of grey were behind him now. He regarded the apple core on the trail with strange affection. He had a good view in every direction, but there was no other sign of the man ahead of him. He wondered if the guy were cold. He himself was. Back to the wind, he sat down on the ridge to eat the rest of his food, but it was too bitter just sitting. It was necessary to keep moving until he reached Iceberg Tarn, which was protected on all sides by higher elevations according to the map.

He did not remember ever being above timberline before, yet the place seemed familiar. The monochromatic tundra; the glacial droppings: gravel, rocks, boulders; the cliffs in the distance—all was familiar. Marmots peered at him from behind boulders like nosy old men. Above, a curious hawk hovered on air currents, the fingers of his wings spread wide. It was one of the earth's boneyards.

They awaited the end of the afternoon shower under a shop awning.

"Looks like she's going to have a blow." Selma pointed to the peak in the distance. As they watched, dark clouds coalesced around it, obscuring it.

"Why she?"

"The usual reason—temperament's unpredictable."

"God, how I hate the thing."

"Now, sweetie, it's just a pile of rock."

The rain stopped in Silver Plume, but the peak remained within the embracing shroud of clouds.

Although the pitch was gradual, the descent to the tarn was treacherous. The trail down the ridge was less than two feet wide in places and dropped off severely on both sides.

After a half hour's struggle, hunched and shivering, he finally reached the tarn. The circle of cliffs provided relief from the wind. He raised his eyes, at last allowing himself awareness of something more than the careful placing of his feet on loose rock.

From the west bank of the tarn, the stone wall reached into the sky. It was bare of everything but streaks of snow and the weather whirling around it. The glacier oozed down a crevasse into the tarn; it was a muted pinkish color. He had never gotten it right in paint. He remembered reading that if you disturbed the surface of some glaciers . . .

He walked around the bank, stretched his foot out, and scuffed the surface snow. That portion of the snow turned scarlet and bled slowly, very slowly, into the tarn.

There were icebergs in the tarn, peaked and graceful like the sails of sloops. The rain turned to snow, although above, deep among the clouds surrounding the peak, he thought he saw glimpses of lightning.

He searched his mind for that French phrase . . . *Déjà vu*. Now he understood the feeling. This place was his dream, the one from which he awoke with fear but without memory. He was almost sure of it. How foolish his horror . . . it was simply this splendid, lovely place.

Scanning the stone wall, he shouted, "Hello, up there. Hello?" A mistake. No one ahead of him. Looking up made him dizzy. Food.

The shelter hut reminded him of an old movie about a POW camp from which attempts to escape were inevitable because what was outside had to be better than what was inside. He ate his sandwich and surveyed the place.

Safety bars on small windows. Bunk beds with torn mattresses. Orange peels and cigarette butts. A rescue

cache containing the paraphernalia necessary for technical climbing. A depleted first aid kit. Several small informative signs.

> UNIFORM DISTRESS SIGNAL
> Three quick repeated calls
> by sight or sound.
> Acknowledgment: two calls.

The fusty smell of the place made him gag on the
sandwich. It was colder in the shelter than outside. Drap-
ing the pack over one shoulder, he left.

The world was a white dervish. For the comfort of a
human voice contesting the argument of wind, snow, and
ice, he shouted, "I prevail in wail and hail." Inching
around the bank of the tarn, he confronted the wall
again. He wanted a more immediate sense of the com-
position of the thing. He found a flat boulder, sat down,
and tried to memorize the face. Unfortunately his sketch
pad was too sodden to use.

One hand instinctively picked up a small stone and
scratched lines on the boulder. The peak rose to a
crescendo of storm clouds.

"Only God knows what will come from such a sky,"
he whispered, laughing.

He blew on his hands. He was one cold boyo—and
tired, too.

Selma said Lucky's was the place to go, because there
you could get eleven different kinds of pizza, beer by
the pitcher, and the music was grand.

A skinny, dour-faced banjo player whose fingers blurred

when he played. An enormous piano player, whose buttocks hung over the round seat. A deboarded upright piano, revealing strings painted with phosphorescence and wired for rinky-tink. Words projected on a screen.

Everyone sang.

Side by side and tea for two and blue heaven . . .

Oh, the old songs were the best, who could or would deny it? Selma's talk became a cadenza.

"Oh yes, he was good—built like one of those bulls—a man and a half, and oh how we'd dance. Come on, Selma, he'd say—sometimes in the middle of the night —and off we'd go to Vegas for the weekend. But then, after the kid came, he started playing around—nothing serious, mind you, just a little here and there, but I got to feeling like an old coat hung on a hook and I let myself go and the blue devils came . . . whump . . . well, well . . ."

Joy put her hand over Selma's wrist. Then they were playing again. "Over the Rainbow." Selma brightened and sang with the rest in a fuzzy but honest bronchial moan that almost got the best of the piano's deliberately corny vibrato.

The Closing of the Gates

They brought him down, tethered on a stretcher, like a hunter's prize.

Exposure, everyone agreed, with muted official satisfaction, as if something had transpired conveniently, even beautifully, with a beginning, middle, and end.

Exposure. Joy mouthed the word several times to get used to it and did not look at Stephen's face.

Mentally, she felt herself all over—as she might after a sudden fall—to see if she were quite whole, asking, what has death done to me?

It mattered, it mattered badly.

Somehow they got her back to Selma's cabin.

"When it happened, what was I doing, what was I thinking, was I killing him in my head?" she asked herself aloud, for lately exasperation sometimes got the best of her, her mind quirked, and she wished violence upon him.

It was important to keep moving, to walk around and around Selma's room.

Later she gave herself up to Selma, let the woman take her and force her to stop walking. Selma was good, kept her mouth shut, and just rocked her. All day and into the night. In the distance Max paced and muttered and Mr. Quick whimpered.

Stephen's parents were contacted. Late the next day his father arrived. He was a small man with a grey moustache and unpleasant eyes. He was displeased with the car he had rented at the airport; he clearly disapproved of them all; but he coped. He had the cash, and his efficiency was astonishing. His weak heart did not impede the progress of arrangements. It took him less than two days to tidy things up.

Joy stayed with Selma—out of his way. When they finally returned to the cabin, they found it stripped of Stephen's belongings. All the canvases were gone except the small painting of Diana's Lake affixed to the back of the kitchen door and thus easily overlooked.

"The stinking bastard!" Selma had been ferocious about Stephen's father from first sight.

"No, no. It was his right. Everything belongs to him." Joy was relieved not to have to face Stephen's things. She put Diana's Lake into a paper bag.

That evening they spoke of the future. Selma and Max said of course she could stay with them as long as she needed or wanted them. "What's ours is yours, little one," Max added gruffly. Joy said, no, she thought it was time to go home. There was her father, after all. They agreed that was probably best, although Lord knows they'd miss her.

Selma was reluctantly persuaded to allow her to spend the night alone in the cabin.

Joy counted what traveler's checks remained in her name, packed her things into the Rueful Hope, and composed a short note to Selma and Max, thanking them and giving them her father's address. Very early the next morning she eased off the emergency brake and let the car roll down the road before starting it up. She'd had enough of farewells.

Stephen said he wanted to see the Oregon coast because someone once told him it was the most magnificent place on earth.

Stephen was being transported to cremation. She disliked morbid curiosity, but still she wondered when, exactly when, they would burn him, precisely when the bones would hit the bin and the smell of burning flesh bring unrest to neighboring dogs.

She twirled the dial, caught Handel on the radio:

"He was despised, rejected, a man of sorrows, and acquainted with grief."

It worked. It made her laugh. It was silly; there was something wrong with the diction or order. Then she missed Stephen most. If he were with her, how he would laugh.

She ran down the beach, her mind screaming above the

stupendous autumn surf—Stephen, Stephen!—until the damp, hard-packed sand came up and knocked her breathless.

Cousin Patricia was there saying, "You can scream all you like for the rest of your life, but nothing will happen."

That night Joy dreamt she was in her father's study. The scroll on the wall glowed. She moved closer to it and read: *Drive your cart and your plow over the bones of the dead.*

The next morning she turned east.

In Chicago she abandoned the Rueful Hope—its transmission was gone—and took a plane. Her last check just covered a cab from the airport to the bus terminal and the fare to her father's house.

She stood for a moment outside the dining room window. The drapes were parted, revealing the table in full array. It gleamed and sparkled by candlelight. Her father raised his glass to the widow of European history.

The feast was within.

With the first snow and the closing of the highest gate on the mountain, Selma departed. Although she usually flew to the coast, this year she had been careless with her alimony. GREYHOUND agreed to take a greyhound provided he was tranquilized.

The second snow closed all the gates. Max's house collapsed, but for perhaps the first time Fortune grinned benignly down upon him. He was away from the house at the time.

TWO

OLD WORLD

Disaffection

Crossing the Boston Common in the late afternoon, Joy laughed at the enormous swan looming with plumed dignity in the distance. It was, of course, only the excursion boat carved in the shape of a swan, left deserted at its mooring on the artificial lake long beyond its season because of some lapse in the bureaucracy of public works. However, the swan's licentious hauteur swelling out of the snow flurries seemed animate. Indifferent to winter, with a self-confident leer, he looked as though he were awaiting the appearance of Leda.

The swanboat kept Joy amused until she unlocked the door of her apartment and walked cautiously through the downstairs hall. Then her mood soured. The place made her feel like the diffident, indigent, and not very competent curator of a small but exquisite museum.

The apartment was sublet from a friend of her father's, an elderly, wealthy art historian now living in Majorca for his health. Although the apartment was large and richly furnished, the rent was minimal, for the old man was more interested in the responsible protection of his *objects d'art* than he was in an income.

In October, when the art historian first called and offered the place, it seemed like a day of miracle in the autumn of disaster. She was back with her public relations firm; commuting from her father's house was tedious, and she felt it was necessary to move out as quickly as possible so that he might get on—unselfconsciously—with his courting. She swore to all the art historian's injunctions about the care and feeding of his rarities and moved into his apartment on the day he vacated it. She had regretted it ever since.

The apartment was not a dwelling, it was an artifice. It smelled of perfect taste and gave her the sense—now, as she stood under the archway leading to the dining room—of permanent dispossession. The mauve walls of the dining room and the intricately gilded ceiling formed a perfect oval; the oval cherry table in the center of the room sat upon an oval Aubusson, subdued but not worn, as were the mauve velvet seats of the delicately carved chairs around the table. A floor-to-ceiling tapestry on one wall bore mythical subjects remote beyond recognition.

It was Cousin Patricia's favorite room. She queened it at the table, a many-emeralded hand extended, waiting to be kissed. Joy turned her back on the dining room, marched past the opulent living room with her face averted, and mounted the stairs to the second floor. Shedding her coat in the bedroom, she sat down at a secretary, stuck a thermometer in her mouth, and leafed through the day's mail. For days she had been feeling neither truly well nor truly ill. The purgatorial in-between consisted of nothing more serious than a dull but persistent migraine, sleeplessness, and a pervasive feeling of unease. The severity of the New England winter and the tedious but relentless office routine might alone account for it. Nevertheless, she checked the column of mercury apprehensively and was relieved when it registered her normality. Then, pulling forward her transistor radio, she switched on WCRB in time for the five-thirty news.

"Southeast Asia . . . Eastern Europe . . . the Middle East . . . A.T. and T. down an eighth, Standard Oil of New Jersey up three quarters . . . Heavy snow predicted by morning . . ."

Historical chaos, financial uncertainty, and bad weather enunciated in mellifluous tones of sweet-tempered candor (nothing got that boy down) gave way to the orderly counterpoint of Scarlatti.

The mail included her renewed passport and a short note from Selma. In two weeks she was off to London for a brief stay, a combination of business and pleasure. It was a bonus of sorts. She was good at her job and, having lost her once, the office now cosseted her.

S.F. was grand, said Selma, and oh when would Joy come for a visit. Joy smiled and drafted an affectionate reply.

In spite of static the radio brought the Scarlatti sonata to its inevitably perfect conclusion, and the phone rang. She knew it was Rolf.

Rolf was handsome in an ordinary way, although the

girls in her office claimed he bore an uncommon resemblance to Paul Newman. Rolf was on comfortable terms with the world and would make a fine stud of a husband for some very clever girl interested in giving birth to superman—if she could catch and keep him. Her own interests were not so focused, but he was company, and she needed company.

"Joy? How are you?"

"Not bad."

"You sound down. What's wrong, dear?"

"The weather, I think. Nothing more."

"Did you have a pleasant Christmas? I tried to reach you, but there was no answer."

"Very pleasant. My father took me to dinner. Thanks for the flowers, Rolf. They're lovely. Still blooming."

Two dozen yellow roses gleamed from a vase on the bedside table.

"Have you decided about our long weekend? We'd better make plans. East, West, North, or South—which will it be? The world is yours."

"Not in only four days, I'm afraid. Let's settle for something quiet and simple. It's really too late for anything else. How about the North Shore?"

"In this weather?"

"Why not, Rolf? The ocean is beautiful at this time of year."

"All right, all right. Whatever you say. It's you I want, anyway, not climate. I'll pick you up on Wednesday around six. You'd better have a drink waiting for me. I'll be fresh—or more likely stale—from a mess of a merger and in need of strong spirits and fond words."

"As you wish, Milord. See you Wednesday."

Scarlatti had surrendered to Viennese waltzes. She turned up the volume and noticed that her wristwatch was stopped. It, too, had been under the weather for days. Ritualistically, she tapped it once against the secretary and twice against the cover of the long-ledger—unopened since Stephen's death. It began to tick again.

Settling into an armchair, she imagined the muffled sounds of Strauss mingling joyfully, like lost spirits having found their rightful world at last, with the Delft tiles, Persian miniatures, Sheridan chairs, and precious Limoges in the art historian's never-never land on the floor below.

Infection

"You're just being silly, you know."

"What *you* don't seem to know—though how you couldn't defies credibility—is that I'm very close to tears. Have you ever seen me cry, Rolf? No, I don't think you have, so you see you know nothing at all of me, for I cry at least twice a week, a fountain, a bath, a geyser of tears, and no, it has nothing to do with the tragic heights or the melancholic depths; it has all to do with nerves. Sheer nerves. Sheer isn't the right word. Knotted and gnarled nerves like roots of trees, veins in the hand . . . oh nerves, alpha and omega . . ."

"That's better. I like to hear you laugh at yourself. Now if you don't want to, Joy, you need only say so."

"But I do want to. Why can't you understand? Oh, God, now I really am crying. Please hand me over a kleenex."

"Here . . . let me . . . wipe away the tears, make it right."

"Don't talk to me as if I were a child, Rolf; I feel foolish enough as it is."

"We're out of joint for a moment, no more, no less. Won't you just lie still and let me make it right."

"But that doesn't do it. You don't know the right from the left of me. It's really incredible. Can't you feel that I don't want you to do that? I should think my skin alone would tell you. I want you in me; I don't want to be primed like some damn pump."

"Quietly now, just relax and stop thinking."

"You sound like a bedside manner. Please, Rolf, just come to me."

Now he shifted—in the name of subtle variety, no doubt, and she felt herself at once ebb, the slow building of her feeling stopped by what he regarded as art and courtesy.

Sometimes it was really impossible to understand why the species went on with it beyond the simple spasm of the male, beyond getting seed where it belonged so that there might be yet another single image of doubled flaws, another generation.

It was going on too long. She could feel his sweat. His wet body moving against her dry body made a curious phlomk, phlomk, phlomk noise which almost brought her to laughter.

Yes, she was willing to admit it: certain fictions clearly drawn in the mind could do the trick in an emergency. Mental pornography. Disgusting but true. The fictional lights on, for example, and the position fictionally complex, while more than one fiction observed. Modified de Sade. As cheap and vulgar as that.

She could hear him laughing. The switch was thrown and he knew it.

It was going to be right, very right, Rolf told himself, in spite of all her nonsense. Luckily her body had its own logic and, luckily, it quite defied whatever it was that went on in her head.

It was a temptation to let go now, but he would hold off. Even if it meant gritting his teeth and thinking about the traffic on Boylston Street at five o'clock, he would hold off.

If it weren't for this—the now of her—he'd settle for an easy lay in one of the one thousand and one accessible landscapes of carnality, for it would be cheaper in expense of psychic energy. But here she was.

"Please leave me now, Rolf. I'm uncomfortable."

"You know, it would be nice if once, just once, we could fall asleep quietly and together."

"Please, Rolf, don't go on and on. Just do as I ask."

"Among women you are the maverick positive. Most women love to continue possession of the male until he wilts beyond the possibility. It's usually the male who wishes to get away immediately."

"Has that been your experience in the past?"

"Oh yes, without exception."

"I thought that was what you liked about me—that I don't clutch after you . . . no clenched jaws of the parasitic womb. Now please . . ."

"You've persuaded me. I shrink, I fade, I leave you. The better it is for you, the more truculent you are afterward. What accounts for that, do you think?"

"I haven't an idea in the world what accounts for that and, furthermore, I don't care what accounts for that. Must we have a postmortem? Is it absolutely essential to dissect the ghost of every moment?"

"It was good for you. I always know when it is good for you."

"You have the queerest, most presumptuous idea that if we twitch and convulse simultaneously, it is, of necessity, good for me."

"It wasn't exactly simultaneous. Yes, that's what I love most. The knowing. Knowing here . . . Knowing there . . . Above all there."

"Don't, Rolf. I don't like to be touched immediately afterward. That's the truth. I like having myself back again. I tell you all the time, but you never listen."

"All right then, I'll just look."

"What in God's name is there to look at?"

"At the body of a woman, of course. Stop talking nonsense. Now what?"

"I just want my robe on."

"What the hell is really the matter? With all your talk, talk, talk, can't you explain in a clear, direct sentence what's wrong? I've never known you so skittish, so edgy as these past two days. It isn't at all like you."

"It's this stuffy, overfurnished room."

"I've never known you to suffer abrasions of sensibility over decor."

"Known, know, knowing—how you go on about it,

Rolf. I've only been . . . with you, if that's the proper euphemism, for a month."

"No, that's not the proper euphemism. You're hardly ever with me. You're certainly not with me now."

"All right, it isn't the room, it's me."

"We are miles apart suddenly, aren't we?"

"Leagues and leagues . . . but still too treacherously close. I think I'll get up and make the distance real."

"Do whatever you like, Joy. During the last two days you've become proof positive of a fundamental precept I've violated."

"And the fundamental precept is . . ."

"Never take an intelligent woman to bed. It's buying trouble."

"I do so agree. Why not an illiterate male for a change —all erection and no dissection?"

"It might be the best thing in the world for you . . . Some jock who would beat the nonsense out of you."

"There's the bedside manner again. The best thing in the world for me right now is fresh air, a long, long walk."

Snow fell on the beach and sea. It was good to be walking, the best thing in weeks. Exercise was what she needed. She ought to take up some sport. Exercise would have her right in no time; she was sure of it.

The consolation was here: nature going on, so beautifully, so simply, so perfectly beyond one. That was all that had ever been said.

Remark the rock, stop the sea-foam at its highest point of reaching—so instructed well-publicized mystics in popular magazine articles on the art of contemplation.

Infection

Doing it at the edge of the sea, with tricks of eye and mind, Joy found that neither the artless solidity of rock nor the spatialized foam provided anything more than ordinary visual pleasantry.

Since Stephen's death, clocks and compasses had stopped; she didn't know where she was. She felt sick all the time and couldn't sleep. It was very like a fever which refused to come to crisis, and yet the thermometer registered nothing at all—another failed dial.

Perversely, she was keeping in sight of the window of their hotel room behind which she imagined were Rolf's eyes. The small, childish part of her hoped he was watching her lone and pathetic figure in ice and snow. She was posing—almost without knowing it, as if she were saying to him: I am crisis, can you not see, will you not come to me? Although if he were to come, she would shuck him off, tell him to go away, mind his own business. Nevertheless, she wanted him to come, to submit to being shucked off.

She trudged on down the beach until the hotel was out of sight and ahead of her a pagoda-like structure rose from the white mist.

The beach house was closed and shuttered. The straight wrought-iron benches surrounding the shelter were blunted with ice. One wanted a companionable circle of benches and fellow beings hunched up and leaning close, not in summer, but in winter when there was the bare-bones necessity for a little animal heat. Here it was —deserted.

Her cloth coat adhered like adhesive to the icy metal bench. She wondered if it was a mistake to sit down when she was already tired and cold, but the walk back would be impossible without a rest. She'd come too far.

She saw an open door leading to a room riper in sunlight than any she would ever know again . . . The supreme clarity of that sunlight . . . And Stephen was saying . . .

No. Memory was dangerous. Winter was a fact.

It was snowing harder. Behind her she could make out nothing but white movement. The way back to the hotel was obscured. It was necessary to move. It was necessary to plant feet firmly on the ground, if feet she still had, and walk.

She recalled what the lady in white once said about grief . . . "Remembered, if outlived, as freezing persons recollect the snow—first chill, then stupor, then the letting go."

She decided to sit on for a while longer; it was the easiest thing to do. Stupor.

"Joy? It's Rolf. Joy, is that you?"

"No one, someone, me, I. It is I. That's correct isn't it? It always sounds so peculiar. Hello, Rolf."

"Hello yourself. Do you realize we're in the midst of what may be the storm of the century and it's getting worse? How long have you been sitting here like this? I've been out looking for you for . . . I don't know how long. Can't see a thing from the road. It's a miracle I found you at all. It's a miracle you're not frozen to death. What the hell do you think you're doing, you idiot?"

"I in the eye of the storm."

"Stop it! I won't listen to any of your nonsense. Come

on, get up. The car's just beyond that dune. Move, damn
you."

"It's so lovely, Rolf, so very white and simple. After
awhile the cold doesn't matter. Please come here and sit
with me for a moment. Please."

"Get on your feet, or so help me, I'll . . . Please
come along, Joy dear. We must get you someplace
warm."

"Very well, I rise and go along."

"There's a good girl. Take care, it's treacherous."

"Take care, take care, walk carefully there."

"Stop talking, Joy, and watch your step."

"Inside, quickly. We've got to thaw you out."

"Like the precooked, cellophane-sealed vegetable, do
not defrost before boiling."

"Oh, very funny, Joy. Sit there on the bed and we'll
get your things off. First, I'm going to pour you a long
drink and I want you to slug it down as fast as possible.
Where the devil is a glass?"

"There's one in the bathroom . . . It hurts, Rolf."

"Here. Drink it down. What hurts?"

"My head."

"That's what you get for going out in freezing weather
without a hat. If you drink that, you won't feel anything
in a matter of minutes. Unbutton your coat."

"I can't. My fingers won't work."

"Never mind. I can manage you."

"This is elixir, Rolf; did you brew it yourself?"

"But of course. Now, give me your feet and let's get
your boots off."

"I can't feel my feet. Those are not my feet; they're someone else's feet."

"Stop playing the fool, Joy."

"Joy's playing a game. She's perfectly sane. That's the name of the game: Joy's playing sane."

"Stop posing. I do know the real from the fake of you. Now, can you manage the rest yourself, or shall I strip you down and bundle you up?"

"You'd better. My fingers still don't work."

"How you shiver. I know my hands are cold. Lift up a bit . . . good. Nightgown in the closet?"

"Yes, on the hook."

"Not much in the way of warmth, is it? You ought to get yourself something more sensible. Put up your arms . . . I wish you'd stop shivering. It worries me. I hope you're not going to come down with anything."

"Could I have some more elixir? It feels good."

"On the spot. Instant potion. I'll even join you . . . The weather is impossible. It's still snowing with a vengeance. God knows when we'll be able to get out of here. Cheers."

"I wish I weren't so cold, Rolf. Not even elixir really does the trick."

"Shall I come close and try to warm you? Think of all my animal heat."

"I do, I do. Continually."

"Just lie still. Quietly, now. That's better, isn't it?"

"Yes, thank you, Rolf. There's much to be said for the small acts of love."

"True, but, Joy, there's something wrong, something I don't understand. We can't go on this way."

Infection

"What did you say?"

"Nothing, nothing at all. We'll talk about it tomorrow. Things will come right tomorrow. They always do. There's nothing to worry about."

"Steady, Joy, just wait a minute while I grab your suitcase. You'll never manage the stairs by yourself. Give me your key."

"I can't seem to find it. Did you ever see such a purse? How I hate clutter. Did it ever occur to you that clutter is the pure form and chaos only the shadow?"

"No, that never occurred to me. Of course you can't find anything—shaking like that. Give me your purse, I'll look . . . Here it is . . . In you go . . . What a mausoleum this place is . . . I don't know how or why you put up with it. It isn't you, Joy; it isn't you. Lean on me . . . Careful, one step at a time . . . Easy. Now get those cold things off and get into bed."

"Stop fussing; it's the flu, not the plague. Rest, liquids. Very simple. Run along home and thanks for the holiday. I'm truly sorry I spoiled it for you."

"Do as I say, Joy, get into bed. I'm calling a doctor."

"No, you're not."

"If you won't give me the number of yours, I'll call my own. We've got to get something into you—penicillin, antibiotics, something—before it gets worse."

"Won't you just run along and let me get some sleep? Flu doesn't give you power of attorney over my life. Next thing I know, you'll be administering extreme unction and letting them cut out my heart for a transplant

. . . all because of a fever and chill. Why are men always such fools about sickness?"

"Here's a couple of aspirin. I'll go make some tea. Try to rest. There's no need to excite yourself."

"Don't patronize me."

"Sleep, Joy, sleep."

She could hear him rattling around in the kitchen below. Somewhere beyond fever and chill, the real world wavered. By closing one eye and squinting the other, she could get the painting on the wall opposite the bed into focus and keep it there for short intervals—Diana's Lake.

Rolf was upstairs again. He was at the phone. She could hear the dial moving, then his damn muttering.

Summer. A very hot day. It was good to think of something warm.

"Light for Joy, wherever she is. Compact, portable, easily placed on any wall . . . the light of this morning."

Stephen had been right. The light of the first morning of the world was still there on the wall opposite.

Patricia, in a floor-length magenta dressing gown, declared from the foot of the bed: "Adam and Eve cut from a synthetic fabric less durable than advertised. The Garden kept by a voyeur."

Who was he, Joy wondered—the man who watched.

The morning light on the wall opposite dimmed and went out.

Rolf's doctor, an old college pal, assured him that most of the city was down with the same thing. Nothing could be done except to ride it out and get antibiotics into Joy in the morning. He promised to stop by first thing and take a look at her.

Rolf hung up the phone, telling himself it was the typical way of his world: he started out for a holiday and ended up with a sick female in a blizzard. There didn't seem to be much point in staying the night. She was asleep now. It had stopped snowing. With luck the car might start.

He stretched, touched his toes once. He had been too long in a closed room breathing the same air—or so it seemed. He might get some skiing in while Joy was abroad. Going on business, she said. Public relations was what her business was called; running errands was what it amounted to. Very expensive errands, he suspected. She was probably making more at it than he was on the lowest rung of corporation law—but that was only temporary.

The truth of the matter was he couldn't keep his hands off her. It was that simple. Even now, just thinking about her . . . There was no explaining it. Eventually they would have to marry and try to make the best of things.

He took the stairs two at a time. He had a strong sense of deserting her, but just as strong was his honest need to do exactly that.

The night air was sharp, fresh, an enormous relief.

Unnatural Spring

"Just like the cold war . . ." Joy later explained to Rolf about the flu. "Weeks and weeks of guerrilla warfare and then finally an offensive and a crisis."

By the time she left for her London assignment she was washed up on the bank of recovery, but also washed out and considerably thinner.

Her firm's client was an international relief organization, and Joy's job was to oversee production of a series of short promotional films for the charity to be viewed on British TV. It was interesting work and work worth doing. The small film company chosen by her firm was very well oiled, and they were able to wind up things in a week, leaving her two weeks of holiday.

Joy decided to spend her first free day walking. She was to have dinner that evening with a scriptwriter from the film company to celebrate the end of their project. She was looking forward to it because, although she knew him only slightly, he reminded her a bit of Stephen.

It was an incredibly mild morning. The parks were alive with mounting mongrels; every dog in London was having his day. Primroses bloomed early.

Her watch had been stopped for three days. Knocking it on wood did not make it tick. Telling the time was a process of induction.

The Trafalgar Square fags were taking the high sun in pairs, arms linked, eyeing with nuances the beautiful boy feeding pigeons in the center of the Square. He was all bird. Only his choirboy's face emerged from the beaks and beating feathers to betray the pleasure he took in bread crumb lust.

The placard on the steps of St. Martin-in-the-Fields announced a concert at one o'clock. There were concerts at St. Martin's on Tuesdays, Joy recalled from a previous visit. The steps of St. Martin's were as yet deserted. Therefore, it was a Tuesday and not yet one. Rewards of the scientific method: she knew the day and the approximate time.

The air announced spring, and it was within her too: a lightness, the heavenly sense of recuperation.

She reminded herself that premature stirrings did not break up all the ice and a January thaw did not bring the small rain. She checked her bag for her collapsible umbrella. Small or large, there would inevitably be rain before the end of the day.

Just like an old maid, she thought—primly fumbling

after an umbrella while sitting in the full and glorious grace of the sun. Nevertheless, it was English weather and she was glad she had the umbrella with her.

She remembered trying to explain to Rolf the first time they met that women were more open to weather, more sensitive to season than men. It was at the end of November, at a party given by her firm in a room furnished after the manner of some legendary brothel.

"And what would you say is the most important difference between a man and a woman, excepting the obvious and delightful one?" he inquired, extending his hand to her in such a way that she could not refuse to take it.

In spite of the atmosphere of debauch she tried to answer the question seriously, saying that women were closer to the earth than men because they were cyclical creatures and nature was cyclical. Rolf accused her of cant, cant as old as the first old wife's tale about her body. He went on to say that most women lied about their bodies, most women cheated their bodies. No doubt he was right.

When she had arrived in London, there were flowers waiting for her from Rolf. Now they were dried up and a subject of distress to the chambermaid, who wished to throw them away. There was much to be said for the small acts of love.

The Square was delightful. With colossal impassivity the couchant lions guarded the ridiculously high pinnacle upon which the Duke of Wellington stood looking to the river and the sea beyond. Fountains erupted and diminished. Joy felt the titillation of their spray on her face. An elderly shopper dozed; the string bag on her lap was filled with the gaudy boxes of the costermongers' age—Kellogg's a long way from Battle Creek. There were somnambulists on all benches, stone steps, and fountain edges. In the sky the words *Bass, Bass, Bass* dangled from a dirigible like a string of droppings from an overfed guppy.

Joy was reminded of Rolf's aquarium, that small universe which subsisted entirely upon his almighty magnanimity, his daily dole of Permalife Salmon Egg Meal. Rolf kept his fishy universe intact with care that even extended to proper control of population. Periodically he removed the water plants in which the newborn hid from the cannibalism of their parents.

As a deity Rolf was a trifle mechanistic for Joy's taste; however, she had to admit that his impartiality was absolute, his fascination with his universe complete; and there was hardly anything more one could ask of a deity. Rolf's faithful observation of the endless repetition in the tank was wonderful. The fish were begotten and born; they ate, defecated, begat, and ate again. Rolf remained enthralled.

Deciding upon the concert at St. Martin's, Joy resisted the indolence of Trafalgar Square and threaded her way among strolling sleepwalkers, who were conscious only of the unexpected warmth of the sun.

St. Martin's was cold and dark. She blinked until her eyes were adapted and walked down the center aisle for a closer look at the richly decorated ceiling.

"By Artari and Bagutti, you know," a voice volunteered. "Quite handsomely done, is it not?" A verger joined her, looking up. His gentle, ethereal face suggested that, for the most part, he either looked up or down, avoiding the danger zone of vision—straight ahead.

She nodded in answer, although she really felt the ceiling was too ornate for the relative austerity of the church.

"One takes it too much for granted," the verger confessed, craning backward, his hands clasped behind his back. "In the winter, when there are so few tourists, we sometimes forget we have it. Handsome indeed!"

"Maintenance must be difficult," she suggested.

"Oh yes, yes," he agreed, still gazing up, as if he were entering a *mea culpa* to the ceiling for his recent neglect of it. "Labor is so dear, you know, and so untrustworthy. Maintenance is a great problem." The verger's head descended from its obeisance to the ceiling. "You've come for the concert, I expect. Just off the center aisle about halfway down is best." He scrutinized the hem of his cassock and then slid away down the center aisle as though perambulating with fins.

Because he reminded her of her father, his face was still in her mind as she relaxed in a pew, but the image of Rolf gradually eclipsed it . . . Rolf in the darkened room, rapt before the long window of his illuminated universe . . .

She remembered Rolf saying that he believed the sexual differences he observed among his fish were valid definitions of the human sexes. The males were lean, swift, nervous, brightly colored. The huge dull matrons of the tank either ate or gave themselves passively, and sometimes did both at once. Their ennui was so complete that even giving birth was a leisurely, disinterested process which did not interfere with the process of eating. Very close to the human condition, for the most part, Rolf said, laughing. Leering comically, he went on to say that of course there were exceptions, beautiful exceptions.

Ingestion, defecation, copulation, gestation: the life of the aquarium never varied, but Rolf went on watching.

Still—there were the small acts of love. After their very satisfactory good-bye kiss in the airport corridor leading to the departure gates, Rolf whispered, "Marry me?" He was as surprised as she by the question. The look on his face was a howl.

The concert was about to begin. Amid scattered applause the pianist and violinist presented themselves with deep bows and took their places. The violinist, a young woman, struck the opening chords. The second piercing note rose to the sumptuous ceiling and lingered. In the tense, wary question and answer of violin and piano it was impossible not to hear the contention of male and female. The young performers, obviously conservatory students, were giving it their all. It was a spirited performance, a follow-the-leader flirtation, with the piano overawed at every point by the high-pitched nerves of the violin. Finally, with an expression of intolerable strain, the violinist brought off the climax of the first movement, a sustained hysterical scream, which was followed by a moment of sweetest harmony and then the reverberations of the denouement.

The second movement was a lullaby-like andante. Time out for some fitful conversation, thought Joy.

They plunged into the presto with barely a pause between movements. The piano was now more assured, more assertive. Passages of frantic staccato smoothed out into long strokes of melody, and then the instruments ranged the scale in rapid ascents and descents until they reached the final frenzy.

The performers disengaged themselves from their instruments with job-well-done smirks.

Joy's exhilaration did not last beyond the door of St. Martin's. There, huddled against a railing, an old woman beat her hands and head on the top stone step, moaning some wordless appeal. The departing audience sidestepped her with eyes averted. The way of the world led sensibly down the steps, but Joy hung back. The head knocking stone reminded her of Selma. Crouching beside the wasted, wailing figure, she was aware that people on the street were looking up at them strangely. She could almost hear them thinking: Doubtless an American, and what does Lady Bountiful think she is going to do with the creature?

"Can I help you?" It was too late to retract her impulse, even though she knew she ought to allow the old woman the freedom and dignity of her eccentricity.

When the old woman did not interrupt her painful dialogue with the church step, Joy asked more urgently, "Is there anything I can do?"

The raised face seemed as old as the stone with which it had communed. The old woman, mouth gaping, shared her mirth with the sky in a long, mocking cackle.

The verger loomed over them. "Now, Sally, that is quite enough. We can't have you making a fuss. I've told you before." Turning to Joy, he said, "You mustn't mind our Sally." With one effortless, proprietary movement he stood the old lady on her feet. She plucked at the sleeve of his cassock coyly and then hobbled obediently down the steps.

"The old hoyden," the verger muttered to himself, smiling, looking up at the sky. "It is not keeping fine. We shall have rain directly. You had better take cover."

Joy realized that the verger was anxious to sweep St. Martin's steps clean of the last scrap of unnecessary, unsightly clutter.

In the torrent of the day's first rain, she hailed a cab back to her hotel. There she napped the afternoon away. The verger, the old woman, Sally, and the pigeon boy joined hands and danced around her in the middle of Trafalgar Square to the tune of "London Bridge Is Falling Down."

Sally and the verger faded, leaving Joy alone with the pigeon boy who suddenly and unaccountably wore Stephen's face. He came closer.

When she awoke she could not remember the end of the dream.

Prologue

Joy was late for dinner with Zac, the scriptwriter.

Zac had suggested Simpson's, and Joy said, no, she'd been to London before and Simpson's before and there was no need for Zac to feel the necessity of Simpson's. He insisted, saying he loved it and was glad for the excuse of an American to go.

Simpson's doorman in a greatcoat complete with golden braid and epaulets helped her from her cab and into the lobby.

During the busy week of filming they had happened on each other frequently but never really looked at each other. They did so now.

Zac smiled warmly.

Joy put out her hand, thinking that for some reason the cragged near-ugliness of the face smiling at her was very attractive. Zac was indeterminately in his thirties and prematurely but gracefully greying. His resemblance to Stephen was a matter of mannerisms rather than features—a certain occasional flamboyance of gesture and speech. She protected herself by erecting a long mental line of skulls and crossbones with red lights illuminating the eye sockets.

"I'm sorry to be late . . ." Joy let the sentence hang, as if there really were a legitimate explanation but one too involved or too personal to be recited in public on such short acquaintance.

The headwaiter guided them to a comfortable corner of the room.

"Whether infested by Americans or not . . ." Zac smiled broadly, "it still serves the best beef in the city."

While Zac ordered, Joy considered the room. It was so carpeted and brocaded as to seem lavishly moth-eaten; it was more lithograph than life.

"Zac for Zachary?" she asked when he turned from the menu to her.

"Zac for Zacharias, father of John the Baptist. According to Testament, he was struck dumb because he refused to believe the angel of the Lord. Joy for Joyce?"

"Joy for Joy."

"That belongs on a scutcheon, imprinted on a banner supported by two unicorns rampant."

A waiter rolled a cart up to their table, exposed a large side of beef, and carved with liberal skill.

"Now that does look splendid."

They chatted about the week's filming. They were amused by some of the same things, they agreed about some of the same people, they pleased each other.

When the waiter cleared the plates, Zac impulsively reached across the table and gripped Joy's wrist. "How long will you be here?"

"A fortnight," Joy replied, wondering if Zac thought love affairs were usually born between the cheese board and the demitasse.

"What do you plan to do with your fortnight?"

"Frankly, I've made no plans. I think I'll spend an aimless fortnight. I think I'd like that best."

"There's this party tonight . . . Please come. We could talk . . ."

Joy allowed herself to be persuaded, and a half hour later they arrived at a town house in Bloomsbury which had known loftier days. Its immaculate facade gave way to a neglected interior.

The room was exactly the sort Joy disliked with active discomfort. It looked like a curio shop on the verge of bankruptcy. A ground floor flat of Babel. Imbroglio of colored shawls, antimacassars, large carpets depicting Oriental beasts upon which were laid small rugs displaying floral bouquets. Hysteria of bowls, boxes, cushions, Madagascar ottomans, and camel saddles. The aromas of incense burning on a miniature altar, Turkish tobacco, marijuana, and eucalyptus branches in a vase.

The atmosphere was really neither mod nor camp because the inmates had been born too soon. Having flowered in the fifties, they were wilted before the coming of the mainstream of modern gaiety. Perpetually, they tried to catch up with rumors of what was new. They wandered uneasily the short distance from restrained hilarity to restrained high seriousness and back again.

Prologue

The busy barrenness of the place was discouraging; Joy wanted to leave.

"Zac, I think I'll just grab a cab back to . . ."

He held on to her.

"You can't do that, you've only just come. 'Yankee manners,' everyone will say. 'Typical American.' The already dark image will be blacker. Repercussions international: marches on your embassy, vandalism at the Hilton, a boycott of goods . . ."

Joy laughed in spite of herself. "Nevertheless, a dull party is a dull party. One has to take a stand."

"Take a chair instead and you may have my vow it won't be dull." With a firm hand on her shoulder he persuaded her into an armchair. "Wait here while I find some refreshment. Then we can talk."

When he reappeared with glasses, he perched on the arm of her chair. "There's that ass Ben, at it again," he muttered.

A sallow young man circled the room with a camera, looking for prey.

"Fear's what I want. Give me the fear in your eyes!" he cried. Intermittently a flashbulb went off, suggesting that he had found it.

He finally came their way and stood square in front of Joy.

"Yank," the errant photographer announced before she spoke. "No fear here."

"Leave, Ben. Just leave." With an autocratic gesture Zac waved him away.

"What's he up to?"

"Just what he says, unfortunately. A photographic essay . . . eyes . . . eyes full of fear and dread. It's just that bad. He only wants natives, so don't be insulted because he didn't take your picture. The fear must be European. He's just a fool."

"I'm relieved, not insulted."

"You don't like having your picture taken?"

"I'd rather go to the dentist. Do you notice how everyone rhymes?"

"No, as a matter of fact. Does everyone rhyme?"

" 'Ben's at it again.' 'No fear here.' Yes, everyone rhymes. It's a sign of the times. You just don't listen."

"I do listen. Listening's my work."

"Oh God, I forgot. You're a writer."

"Is that bad?"

"Not bad, just predictable. It's one of the hazards of the milieu. When you're not scripting promotional things, what do you write?"

"Plays. I've just had one on."

Joy was amused because Zac was being defensive, telling her that his writing was serious stuff, and successful, too—not a mere amateurish accident having to do with his milieu. He, like Stephen, took his work too much to heart.

"I am, in fact, just about to take another play on tour . . ."

As if suddenly hearing the ludicrous solemnity of his words, Zac laughed, and recanted.

"Actually, the play I'm taking on tour is strictly an experiment and certainly nothing to boast of. Speaking of tours, you're a tourist and ought to have one. Whom of our gay assembled company would you like to meet? And very gay it is, I fear."

"No one. Why don't you just tell me about them instead?"

"Super. Where would you like me to begin?"

"With the glorious lad at the feet of that evil old man." Joy indicated a Greekly beautiful young man sitting on the floor with his head against the knees of a bald man playing a zither.

"Ah yes, that is Timothy. He does catch the eye, doesn't he? I know exactly what you're thinking. You're thinking it's a pity all that . . ." Zac pointed surreptitiously at Timothy, "should be wasted. It's the predictable female reaction. Timothy's color is a bit high tonight, a bit livid, because he's been out the whole day, in the rain, picking berries on Hampstead Heath. It seems there are berries on Hampstead Heath, although what they're doing there is anyone's guess. Timothy is certainly a child of nature—picking berries from morning 'til night."

"Does he do it for love or for money?"

"A little of both. He's really a very nice moron. More interesting by far is Timothy's evil old man, that poor bald penguin. He was once something of a figure, a man of gifts and parts, a short-lived lion. Now it's the zither and a succession of Timothys. Sad. Grievous sad. Also of interest are our exotic host and hostess, a charming couple from Pakistan. Unfortunately, they don't seem to be here. Very odd. Everyone else is a bore, except myself, of course . . . Wait, wait . . . I have forgotten someone after all. There—the fellow collapsed against the wall, scowling at you. Llewelyn, called Lew."

Joy confronted the scowl. A jealous scowl, she decided, although Lew was too far away for her to be sure.

"Lew waits to be beckoned, so beckon I will," said Zac. "You mustn't mind Lew; he's always roily. It's partly his work. He's a journalist, you see. A good one, I'm told, although I can't read his stuff. He does a weekly column out of London for a paper in Wales. Lew's very Welsh."

Lew presented himself. He gave an impression of Welsh bagginess familiar from photographs of the gone-to-seed Dylan Thomas.

"Lew has to do with the play I'm taking on tour," Zac explained.

"What's it about?"

"It's about your war," Lew replied.

"My what?"

"Steady on, old man," Zac said firmly. "You've no call to be rude. On and on, day after day . . . if it isn't FREE WALES, it's PEACE. PEACE IN OUR TIME. Even you, Lew, have got to admit that the idea is hardly spanking with originality. Truthfully, old man, I've been rehearsing since early morning and I'm sick of the bloody subject—no pun intended."

"Zac's written a very good play," said Lew conciliatorily.

"And it's the play I'm concerned with, and only the play. I leave social conscience to Lew here. He's got enough for both of us—with surfeit to spare. The play's a rather interesting experiment. It takes place sometime

Prologue

in the future when England is wired for civil defense with all manner of alarms and sirens. It's set in a school-room and the cast consists entirely of children, with the exception of the schoolmaster, a wild-eyed chap who's very advanced for the village. I'm playing his part myself. He gives lessons in spelling, mathematics, and history, but they all really have to do with the war; in fact, any war, all war. The script's no more than a collection of questions and answers. Most of the action is improvised. The order of the lessons and the questions is different every time we rehearse. The children respond to me, to the things I say, as they would in a live school-room. Because the play is constantly changing, it's as real to them as anything in life. I've got six of them: three boys and three girls between six and ten years old, borrowed from one of those very progressive schools. I taught there for awhile, so they've lent me the children. They're beautifully responsive. We're completely self-contained. We'll be going about in a van—the seven of us. Just a few scraps for props, a tape recorder, and a movie projector. It's a marvelous experiment. Lew's got a foundation to put up the money. We're going to try it out in Windsor, Oxford, and Cambridge. You ought to meet my brood, Joy. You'd like them. Anyone would. They're far superior in every way to adults. In fact . . ." Zac considered her with an appraising look. "You'd better come with us. The brood needs a woman."

"You must be mad!" Joy exclaimed, while admitting to herself that Zac's improbable idea was tempting.

Llewelyn, still planted in front of them, was visibly relieved at her response.

"No, not mad at all," Zac protested. "To the contrary. I'm becoming more convinced by the minute that it's a superb, a brilliant idea. A woman of sound sense from distant parts—exactly what the brood and I need, and I shall convince you. Just wait and see."

Obviously uncomfortable, Lew bowed slightly to Joy and said in a proprietary voice, "See you later, Zac?"

"Not likely," Zac replied, resisting the claim.

"As you will." Lew returned to his wall and with studied absorption began scribbling in a pocket notebook. "Sullen Llewelyn . . . that's almost a rhyme. He's rather too attached to you, isn't he, Zac?"

"Yes, but not I to him."

"I didn't think so."

They talked about music, they talked about books. They both felt it was good talk. When they left the party, they took a cab to her hotel.

Zac was obviously delighted with the place. "How did you ever find it? What a monument to the solid, well-fed life. Old England."

"I happened on it my first time here. It's nice. The population is neither overwhelmingly American nor too stolidly British, but rather predominately French and German. Consequently, there's no need to keep up conversation at breakfast. The eggs are always overdone, but the sausage is delicious. I like solid furniture, circular stairs, and high ceilings."

"Old England rented out; what a melancholy thought. Ah, but there's a lounge and the lounge is open. Let's have a nightcap."

"Bitter. I haven't yet had any this trip."

Prologue

"Sit here and I will fetch."

He returned with half-pint mugs. "These are surely two of the Empire's last dented silver tankards. And now, tell me what your life is like."

"What a request. I suppose I have an obligation to be clever. Let's see now . . . my life . . . a shack of a thing, more durable than straw, but less than stone. I have nightmares about acts of God against which I'm not insured: earthquakes, whirlwinds, wounds without cause, sudden deaths, the unexpected beast which is never very far away, prowling, threatening to huff and puff and blow the house down."

"The same might be said for all of us. Surely there's more."

"There's my job, as you know. I'm a kind of woman-of-all-work for the place. It's sometimes interesting and I'm reasonably good at it. For the most part, I'm content to give the dingy universe a peek from behind cretonne curtains, although I admit I envy Llewelyn his causes and you your plays."

"Come be a part of my play. I was serious when I first asked; I'm even more serious now."

"Close myself in a van with you, six children, and a play? You must admit the idea sounds ridiculous."

"Just think, lodgings and food are provided, and the charm of rural England as well, if the weather keeps fine. I'm an expert driver and there's the advantage of my company, for I'll do everything I can to keep you amused —and don't forget the Cause: awakening slumbering minds to the bitterness of their treachery, their abnegation of responsibility. According to Lew, that's what the play's all about. Just think: two weeks of The Bell Tolls for Thee. What could be more entertaining?"

"Cause or not, it sounds like a proposition pure and simple, if propositions are ever pure and simple." Laughing, Joy led the way from the lounge to the lobby.

"I shall have to make you fall in love with me. It's a pity I have only two days to do it in. We leave in two days you see. I'll pick you up here tomorrow immediately after rehearsal, about half-past five. Two days. I haven't a moment to waste."

Zac blew her a kiss.

Joy slept immediately. The long corridor on the third floor of the house led to a gallery. The gallery itself was dark, but each of the enormous paintings was illuminated.

A brass plate bore the title of the first painting: *Sea Forms*. A diver under water. She knew before she approached that the diver was Rolf, even though he was obscured by goggles and burdened with oxygen tanks. Surrounded by starfish, conch shells, and coral and waving a trident, Rolf was jocund. He mounted a large sea turtle and sailed to the foreground. Joy moved quickly away from his watery world.

The second painting was a garden scene in baroque dress. The verger of St. Martin's was ornately garbed in scarlet with a tall bishop's hat. Selma, her hair piled high, her bodice immodestly loosened, stooped to kiss first his ring and then the hem of his robe. The verger became Joy's father. He raised Selma up gently and they began a slow, intricately figured dance. Crouched against the trunk of a mulberry tree, the wizened old woman, Sally, in peasant rags, plucked the strings of a lute with withered fingers. Selma and her father danced a minuet in the garden of an ancient spring.

"Eleven o'clock, ladies and gentlemen. Closing time. Eleven o'clock." The epauleted doorman, a clarion tucked under his arm, marched down the gallery. "Eleven o'clock. Closing time."

Joy walked anxiously to the end of the gallery and the last painting. Stephen was there. She put her hand to his lips and when he did not respond she bent forward to kiss him. Then his hands moved tenderly along her arms and brought her into the painting and away from the voice coming closer: "Closing time."

She was crying with relief, unable to speak, and the man called Zac was suddenly the figure in the painting and he was saying, "You'll come with me, won't you?"

Zac did not sleep. He paced along the Embankment. There was something about Joy he hadn't quite got hold of yet.

He turned and faced into the mist rising from the river.

It was beginning again, that was it. He banged his fist against the base of Cleopatra's Needle. He was going to write about her, that was it. Unable to contain the relief he felt, he began to run.

He had written his first play joyfully, explosively, almost unaware of what he was about. When it was produced, he chucked his teaching job and took part-time work with the film company in order to get on with his writing. But nothing came. Nothing except the children's play which was no more than an experiment—amateur gymnastics.

Now it was beginning again.

Zac ran along the edge of the river until he could run no more.

The new moon held the old moon in her arms—as in the old ballad. There was some superstition . . . He couldn't remember what it was.

Child's Play, Act One

The sudden spring—a shot in the dark of more natural winter—spent itself. It rained unceasingly for two days and snow was predicted for the highlands.

Joy caught sight of Zac, in mackintosh and boots, searching the post-breakfast crowd in the lobby. She waved and he coiled his way toward her around clumps of people. A shaving cut on his chin was ineptly patched with a piece of tissue.

"Bitter morning . . . bitter, bitter. London is all ice. It's possible to skate from here to Piccadilly. Could you do with a skate, Joy? The roads would challenge a sled. You're in for a harrowing journey. Perhaps the new ice age is finally upon us—the coming of the Arctic pack."

He stooped to kiss her; his cold face burnt her cheek.

"Is this your case? Come along then, it's time for you to meet the brood. I'm wrongfully parked directly in front of the hotel . . . You see what I mean about the weather. Beastly climate. I can't imagine why anyone stays, why anyone comes. From summer to winter in forty-eight hours. It's positively unhealthy. Shall I spread my mac gallantly or can you totter along without? Careful, don't slip. I'll just throw your case in the back. How quiet you are this morning."

"But Zac, you haven't left me the space necessary to say good morning in."

"Good morning, dear Joy. Tell me, what do you think of our chariot?"

"Just about the strangest vehicle I've ever seen. Where on earth did you get it?" The car looked like a hybrid mingling of an American station wagon and an English caravan.

"Lew dug it up someplace. We've been sharing her for more than a year now."

The name came as a surprise. In the past two days, Zac's disciple had been absent both in the flesh and in conversation. Joy had almost forgotten him.

Small faces peered at her from behind the rain-drenched windowpanes.

"Take care of the curb . . . in you go."

With a comforting hand on her arm, as if she were about to face something formidable, Zac made the introductions.

"Left to right: Anna and Alec; Christopher, Dawn; Iris and Derrick, you can't go wrong. You see, I've arranged them in rhyme to make them easier for you to remember. You have such an ear for rhyme. Children, this is Joy."

Child's Play, Act One

With a stagy downbeat, Zac led the children in a choral response:

"Good morning, Joy."

Twisting around in the front seat, she smiled at them. She glimpsed brooding metaphysics on the far left—presumably Anna—and mischief on the far right—Derrick according to the rhyme. Slumped disconsolately against Anna was a panda, life-size but eyeless. The four crowded figures between Anna and Derrick presented a blurred aura of wise child. All six stank of precocity.

"Their parents must trust you to let them out like this," Joy whispered, testing the possibility of adult conversation sotto voce.

"Their school, not their parents, 'lets them out,' as you put it. It's very progressive. Experience: the great teacher, you know; creativity must be nurtured. Covent Garden once a week and safaris in Africa during holidays. Communal nude bathing for sex education. Filthy rich and very advanced."

Zac started the van and under the cover of the revving engine added, "I have not introduced you to the seventh, who is always beside them—Anna's companion. Wither Anna goest, the bear goes too. It's eyes were loose for a long time. They were affixed to its head by long pins and, fearing an injury, one of the mistresses insisted upon removing the eyes this morning . . . without benefit of anesthesia, I'm told. The scene has the true tragic ring: 'out vile jelly!' Both Anna and the bear have, this very morning, confronted inexorable fate and gone down. For the moment, Anna is inconsolable. The bear, I expect, makes the best of it. I have not introduced you to panda because although he does have a name, only Anna knows it. Like the Tetragrammaton, the bear's name is too sacred to be uttered. I must admit I'm pleased with the thing; it goes on stage and adds poignancy to the performance."

"Damned silly, I say." Derrick had been straining his ears to catch Zac's drift.

"Zac, please ask Derrick not to be profane," said Anna primly. Derrick and Anna, mischief and metaphysics, were the poles of personality and natural enemies.

"Anna's quite right, old man," Zac addressed Derrick in the rear-view mirror. "For all we know, panda may be a very sophisticated companion."

A shrill voice announced, "I agree with Derrick. It's silly at Anna's age to have a bear wherever you go."

Joy identified the voice as belonging to Iris, sitting next to Derrick. Obviously the girl had eyes for the boy. Iris was a gawky, black-haired child who looked older and nastier than the rest. Although lacking the courage to cast the first stone, no doubt she would always be more than willing to cast the second or third. She was mischief's perfect consort, although mischief seemed indifferent to her presence.

"I had a panda once, Anna. I still remember him fondly," Joy said.

Arms folded grimly, Anna stared out the car window from behind National Health Service steel-rimmed glasses, refusing to be consoled.

Joy gave the matter up.

"Just how old were you when you had the panda?"

The voice of reason belonged to Alec—very chubby,

with the fat boy's desire to keep things peaceful. Alec
bore the physical discomfort of Anna's despair pressed
against his right side and, on the other, most of the
burden of a slumbering angel—Christopher, according to
Zac's rhyme—who seemed to be the youngest.

"I really don't remember, Alec," Joy replied.

"You don't remember?" Alec echoed with disbelief.
"Would you say you were older or younger than Anna
is now?" He seemed determined to get to the bottom
of the panda affair by means of the Socratic method.

"I'm sorry I can't answer you, Alec, but I really don't
remember how old I was then and, of course, I don't
know how old Anna is now," Joy said with logic as
punctilious as his.

Anna kept disdainfully silent.

"That's just like old Alec, always saying something
that hasn't got anything to do with anything," sneered
Derrick.

Alec opened then closed his mouth, apparently deciding not to risk himself in further defense of a point that
was moot. His worried, baffled expression was that of the
habitual scapegoat.

"Yes, that's exactly like Alec," said Iris, the shrill
shrew. Her teeth were wired and she looked like a horse.
Joy prognosticated an English old-maidhood for her. Iris
would neigh flattering agreement all her life, but mischief would never have her.

All six children were perfect specimens for the old
game of types, Muffin, Horse, and Bird. Alec, with his
mounds of baby fat, was the quintessence of muffin.
Anna was the strange and delicate bird. Both Iris and

Derrick were horse: Iris, the ugly mare; Derrick, the high-spirited colt with an appropriate mane of red hair. Christopher and Dawn were bird-muffin and clearly brother and sister. Dawn, slightly older than her brother, was the flapping robin fussing over her fledgling.

Sensing the drift of public opinion, Dawn put a careful arm around Christopher and removed as much of his sleeping form as possible from the proximity of Alec's offending bulk. Christopher, obviously used to such handling, did not wake.

Zac was relieved to find the Great West Road ice free and the van's heater working for a change. He was also pleased with Joy's response to the children. Except in the matter of the play, his consistent policy with them was one of observation without intervention, and Joy seemed willing to share that attitude. As they passed Heathrow, one of the transatlantic BOACs was just landing, and she described her own flight to the children. Nothing forced, nothing elaborate, simply a gesture of her goodwill. She would keep natural with them, that was the important thing.

Joy's profile was etched on the periphery of his vision as he remembered Lew turning over the van's keys to him that morning and asking in a hard, tight voice: "Why are you involving yourself with that person?"

He had replied without thinking, "Because she's a beautiful woman." It still seemed the right answer to the question, but the nature of its rightness was not simple. It was the right answer to Lew, for if Lew deliberately avoided the sexual note with the neuter phrase "that person," it was necessary to insist upon it with the phrase "beautiful woman." If Lew chose to dog his heels with domesticated loyalty, offering up unrequited passion on a platonic salver, it was necessary to remind Lew that the loyalty and the passion were unsolicited, undesired, and consequently imposed no obligations. If he wanted the woman, he'd take her. Lew had to understand that it was none of his damn business.

However, Zac knew that when he used the word "beautiful" he wasn't really naming Joy—a well-formed, pretty, rather sad girl—but his extraordinary excitement with his idea: a short story or another play—as yet he couldn't be sure what form it would take—based in part upon something that had happened light-years in his past. He couldn't have been more than four or five years old at the time. His family had an *au pair* girl living with them, a Czech student studying at London University. One night she came to his room, lay down next to him, and murmured to him for hours in her native language, until sleep defeated his uneasiness. Shortly thereafter she disappeared quite inexplicably from the family. Years later he realized her strange visit and her disappearance had coincided with the Munich Crisis. Although he wasn't sure why, Joy reminded him of the Czech girl. Perhaps it was the odd shadow of isolation she cast.

With much less than half his mind on the road, Zac rehearsed his idea. He wanted to write about an affair between a Czech girl and an Englishman during the Munich Crisis. He wanted to emphasize the isolation of two people in an emotional no-man's-land at a time when the pressure of events was powerful in the extreme.

He wanted to show how events invaded and private life came to reflect the nature of events.

He suddenly saw that it wouldn't do as a play. A story. He'd wait and see how it spun itself out. The first sentence was already there.

The basement flat had but one window.

"Left turn for Windsor." Zac read the sign aloud. "We're almost there."

Joy did not respond. Cousin Patricia was accusing her of having no will at all, of drifting with the first current, the first pockmarked European. Surrounded by one man, six children, rain, and a tragic panda, she could not possibly be in her sane and perfect mind, according to Patricia.

"Cragged, not pockmarked," Joy corrected.

The children prevented further interior debate.

"Zac," Derrick called out, "remember you promised!"

"Promised what, old man?"

"To decide who was to die."

"Oh Zac, you didn't forget, did you?" Dawn joined in.

"I most certainly did not. I've been giving the matter long and careful deliberation." Grinning, he explained to Joy, "You see, at the end of our play there's a death scene, a very rum death scene, and as yet I haven't said who's to play it."

"Choose, Zac!"

Joy gathered that the death scene was of first importance, for even the angelic Christopher, still at rest in the arms of Dawn, roused himself.

Child's Play, Act One

"It won't be me," Christopher said with a less than angelic whine. "I never get to do anything important because I'm youngest."

"That's right, Christo, it's not going to be you," Zac said. "But age has nothing to do with it. Talent's what we need. Anna dies best. She has the true fatal gift. I've decided Anna's to die."

"Oh no," groaned all but Anna and Alec. Anna was transported from sulk to delight, while Alec remained benign, as if he had known all along that the honor of dying was hopelessly beyond him.

"A girl will never do it right," Derrick complained.

"I think Derrick would be splendid. Ever so much better than Anna. Really, I do, Derrick," Iris repeated in case he should doubt her sincerity.

"Zac doesn't agree," grumbled Derrick.

"No, he doesn't, and that's an end to it," laughed Zac. "Anna's going to die. Settle down now. We're just about there."

The promise of death improved Anna immensely. She turned her attention from the blind bear to Alec and began to tickle and punch him. Sadly resigned, Alec tried to ignore her. Joy wanted to tell the neurotic little brat to leave him alone.

Zac whispered, "There's nothing to be done about it. It's the way of the world. He sticks it pretty well."

"He shouldn't have to."

"He's got dignity, our Alec has. Mustn't interfere."

"*Our* Alec? Really Zac, I will not serve *in loco parentis,* I simply won't. I'm just a tourist along for the ride."

"Just a way of speaking. Don't be so thorny, love."

In Windsor, Lew's foundation had booked them into a hotel overlooking the castle: two triple rooms for the children and two singles for themselves with connecting doors between the rooms.

Perhaps guessing her sympathy for him, Alec was the first to knock at Joy's door. He planted himself in front of her and announced: "Zac says you're his very special friend."

"In that case, Alec, I certainly hope that any special friend of Zac's is a special friend of yours, because I'm sure we'll be seeing a lot of each other."

Joy hesitated to think just how complete Zac's explanation of the phrase "special friend" might have been. The school the children came from seemed more advanced than Summerhill and more than faintly corrupt.

Iris was next on the scene.

"What a smashing dress! I just love purple."

Joy winced and continued to unpack until Zac arrived and ushered them all down to lunch.

After lunch Zac and the children went to rehearse in a cellar at Eton recently converted to an experimental theater.

Joy took a walk down the High Street, met an elderly man with Churchillian jowls and a Yorkshire terrier, and chatted briefly about the wretched weather, the scarcity of tourists in winter, and the unfortunate long-range effects of devaluation. Back in her room she puttered with laundry and with the lady poet—still unread. Finally she wrote three postcards. For Selma in San Francisco: "Piccadilly Circus by Night"; for Max in Sante Fe: "The

Changing of the Guard at Buckingham Palace"; and for her father: "The National Gallery."

Dearest Father, I am well. The weather here is dreadful although just two days ago it was like spring.

She contemplated sending her best to the widow, but she was unsure of the spelling of her name. Instead she simply signed off with a large *Love, Joy.* She had already written Rolf to thank him for the flowers, and her office about the completed films. She tried Zac's door, found it unlocked, and wandered in.

It was clear that Zac liked leather. His elaborate cowhide suitcase, with its assortment of straps, pockets, and dividers, and a shaving kit of kid were the only sign of luxury in the room. On the small writing desk there was a piece of hotel stationery upon which he had written in pencil:

The basement flat had but one window.

Suddenly Zac was behind her as she bent over the desk.

"So here you are." He seemed neither surprised nor annoyed to find her there. "I just tried to knock you up. I thought perhaps you were having a nap."

"Knock me up? That's a very vulgar phrase in Americanese."

"Knock you up as in rouse you is what I meant, rouse you to tell you that we're back and the brood have gone dutifully to their rooms for a wash."

Zac stretched out on the bed, hands behind his head. "What a rigorous afternoon we've had. What perils I have known, what sights seen, since last we met. Poor Anna has died at least twenty times. An Etonian moron hopelessly tangled the tape, and in my little masterpiece the tape is all, the very heart of the drama, the *deus ex machina* as it were. Then the projector blew a fuse, and Anna could not be made to die an ordinary death. She's devilishly self-conscious about dying today: Bernhardt or nothing, and it's far too late to give the part to one of the other children for tonight's performance. It's a very difficult problem. I can't very well ask Anna to cultivate her 'affective memory.' After all, she's never died before, has she? And what have you been doing, love, all this long afternoon?" Zac at last petered out.

"Just now I've been looking at your things," she confessed. "Isn't that awful? I'm glad you're back."

She went to him and he took her in his arms.

The Eton cellar looked like a medieval dungeon recently and almost successfully beseiged by an inexpensive decorator from Chelsea. Zac expressed concern that the translucent mobiles and basket chairs arranged in a semicircle might mitigate the atmosphere of his play. He and the children retired to an anteroom to give Anna's death one last dry run.

Joy watched the small audience assemble. There was an assortment of Etonians in their peculiar garb and a number of the haughty, hawkish women, so familiar to the school setting, who prided themselves on patronizing the avant-garde in more ways than one.

The two chairs in front of Joy were claimed by a large, bosomy woman and her companion, a youthful, long-haired cadaver. Their relationship was made uncomfortably clear by the woman's overt display of possession.

She demanded the rearrangement of her coat across her shoulders, the lighting of her cigarette, the fetching of an ashtray, and finally the holding of her hand, as she leaned toward the young man and began a whispered monologue audible to all around them, the disconnected account of luncheon with a friend: "Darling, you know what Vickie is, the least thing upsets her, and so you can imagine the state she was in. Charles simply walked out, giving the feeblest excuse in the world. He said he was going to Malvern to purchase parts for that Morgan of his and wouldn't be back until the weekend."

"Well, darling, it's just possible that he's gone to do exactly that," said the young man. "The Morgan's a difficult motor to fit out. Overhead valves, you know. Vickie's too suspicious."

"My sweet, *you* are too naïve. We both know they've been having difficulties and I'm the first to agree that Vickie's really to blame. If only she'd keep Charles on a longer leash. I've told her countless times . . . But surely you can't really believe he's gone off in the middle of the week, without leaving her an address, simply because of that wretched car."

"But you know Charles is fanatical about sportscars. It's just the sort of thing he'd do—rush off to Malvern with hardly a word."

"Its an obsession with him, you're quite right there. I've told Vickie more than once that I thought it extremely unhealthy, but Vickie won't listen. What she sees in Charles I can't imagine. He's such a dreadful bore. Anyway, she's sure he's gone for good. By the time dessert arrived she was in tears. I didn't know what to say to her. It's all so very pathetic. We must all rally round poor Vickie, really we must. You've no idea how depressed I am. I can't get my mind off her weeping, her mascara dripping into the trifle. I don't know why it should upset me so, but it has."

"Not to worry, darling," said the young man with indifferent kindness. His fingers, entwined with the woman's, toyed with her large diamond ring.

Joy shuddered, thinking that Selma was certainly right about life being seepage; look where you ended up, if you let it get the best of you. Joy looked again and shuddered again.

"So here you are." Llewelyn suddenly materialized like a demon out of air. "May I sit next you?"

"All right," Joy replied reluctantly. Although Lew was sadly comical, with his high seriousness and his pitiful attachment to Zac, she was resentful of his presence. Obviously he had followed them to keep a jealous eye on Zac.

As if divining her thought, Llewelyn explained somewhat defensively, "Zac went off without these." He pointed to a pile of mimeographed sheets. "They are to be distributed after the play."

"Propaganda?"

"No. Common sense. This war has got to be stopped. Surely you can see that. The foundation does not believe in propaganda; it believes in education."

"I see. The old soft sell."

"Pardon?"

"Nothing. Tell me about this foundation of yours."

"There's very little to tell. It's a hodgepodge of people

really. All ages and classes. People who care about what's happening, people who are concerned."

"Frankly, that sounds very vague."

"Ah yes, I've been forgetting how you Americans like things named—all labeled up tidy. The foundation hasn't any firm political affiliations, but for convenience' sake, I think we might say that its philosophy is left of Labour, slightly right of the C.P. You must remember we haven't the terror you Americans have of the extreme left. We're a small country, caught between the devil and the deep blue sea, and, in our case, beyond the deep blue sea there's yet another devil. All we're concerned about is peace. This madness must stop now, in our generation."

"Oh now really . . ." groaned Joy.

Eavesdropping on the distressed matron was far more amusing than listening to Lew. Fortunately, the play began.

Led by Zac, the children filed in, pair by pair, arranged according to height—Christopher and Dawn, Anna and Alec, Derrick and Iris—singing "God Save the Queen," accompanied by a brass band on the tape recorder. The audience stood until the anthem was completed.

The set consisted of six worn student desks, their gouged-out graffiti visible from a distance, and a blackboard. The backdrop presented a large window behind which was a movie screen. A rural landscape—pasture and Tudor farmhouse—was projected on the screen.

While Zac wrote on the blackboard, the children portrayed typical restlessness in the face of lessons. Anna, with her bear bundled beside her, tormented Alec. She tickled the back of his neck with a ruler; when he squirmed to avoid it, she poked him in the ribs. Alec had such a look of buffoonish helplessness that he practically brought down the house. His was the innate pathos of the gifted clown. While he writhed and mugged, Derrick created a squadron of paper planes and sent them on mission after mission. The target was always Zac's back, and finally one hit its mark. Christopher gasped with fear, Iris tittered uncontrollably, Derrick assumed an expression of innocent calm, and Zac turned around, tapping his pointer severely on Alec's front row desk, striking dangerously close to one chubby hand.

"Children, you will come to order this instant!"

Quiet descended upon command. Exercise books were opened, pencils dutifully poised.

"We shall begin our lessons this morning with words. Spelling and definitions." Zac tapped the blackboard upon which he had written: *Important Words We Should Know.*

"Let us begin with a simple three-letter word which denotes one of man's most important and complex activities." Zac paused and the audience laughed.

"W-a-r," Iris spelled, rising by her desk.

WAR, Zac wrote on the blackboard with red chalk.

"And where does the word come from?"

Derrick stood and recited with exaggerated pedantry: "From the Middle English and Old Norman French *werre*, meaning to sweep or drag. Exact sense development of the word is unknown."

"And what do we mean when we say the word?"

"War: the art, activity, profession, or science of military operations; the methods and principles of warfare," recited Anna, one hand clutching the panda's ear.

"Ah yes, the principles of war. Before we have done, we must hear more about the principles of war." Zac pointed to Dawn.

"War: any active hostility or contention; conflict; strife," she chanted.

Christopher, a world-weary cherub, joined in: "That's life . . . all trouble and strife."

Derrick stood and waited impatiently for the laughter to subside.

"War: a card game for children in which the cards are turned up one by one; the highest takes the others and in case of a tie the next turn decides." Facing the audience, Derrick pointed to the movie screen behind the window. "Observe, please."

The pastoral scene was replaced by a children's playground with Derrick and Alec sitting on the ground, turning up cards one by one. The game proceeded evenly until the appearance of the ace of spades and the ace of hearts occasioned a tie. At the next turn, Alec's king of clubs gave him the edge. A close-up of Derrick's face revealed gathering anger. Suddenly he was on top of Alec. He had the advantage of height and agility. Alec remained pinned beneath him, forced to endure unmerciful pummeling.

Watching their images on the screen, Alec and Derrick acted out exaggerated responses. Derrick doubled over with hilarity; Alec registered each blow as if he were suffering it anew, mutely appealing to the audience. As their tussle reached its pitch, the film scene changed.

The next sequence lasted only an instant, just long enough for the audience to grasp what it was. Two soldiers, one astride the other, in the same position as Alec and Derrick, struggled for possession of a rifle: Zac and Llewelyn, costumed for World War II.

"Give it him! Go it! More, more!" shouted Derrick and Iris, cheering on the victor. The battlefield quickly faded and the farmhouse reappeared.

From the tape recorder came strains of the "Blue Danube Waltz" and then:

"This is the BBC interrupting your evening program of light classical music to bring you the following public service announcement. This is a test of the early warning system. We repeat, this is a test. In the event of possible attack, the following siren will sound at ten-second intervals. Proceed in an orderly manner to the nearest shelter. We repeat, this is a test."

While three piercing blasts of a siren sounded, the children remained frozen. Then the recorded voice announced: "We return you to the program in progress."

Action resumed.

"And now children," said Zac, "let us consider what we know about this word war. Anna, you may begin."

She stood and the panda tumbled to the floor. She righted him, dusted him off, patted his head, and, after a deep breath, declaimed:

" 'And thine eyes shall not pity, but life shall go for life, eye for eye, tooth for tooth, hand for hand, foot for foot.' " Clenching her fists, closing her eyes, Anna bellowed: " 'Hear, O Israel, ye approach this day unto battle against your enemies: let not your hearts faint, and do not tremble, for the Lord your God is he that goeth with you . . .' " Anna sank into her seat with melodramatic fatigue.

"Jehovah had his sanguinary moments, did he not?" Zac remarked dryly. "And you, young man," he pointed to Christopher who was yawning, "what have you learned about this word *war?*"

"Our Lord, Jesus Christ, has said, 'these things *must* come to pass, but the end is not yet.' " Christopher fidgeted and looked anxiously to Dawn for help.

" 'For nation shall rise against nation,' " she coached.

" 'For nation shall rise against nation, and kingdom against kingdom; and there shall be famines and pes . . . pest . . . pesselences, and earthquakes in diverse places,' " Christopher concluded in a triumphant rush of words.

When the laughter died away, Alec faced the audience. " 'All these are the beginning of sorrows.' " As he spoke, the farmhouse was replaced by a no-man's-land, empty but for an occasional crater and a vast expanse of barbed wire.

"So much for the Prince of Peace," said Zac, causing a ripple of discomfort in the audience.

"Let us consider the word peace, let us consider it carefully."

"P-i-e-c-e," spelled Derrick, with a facetious display of boredom.

"That's enough, Derrick," Zac warned.

"P-e-a-c-e," Anna spelled decorously. "Freedom from war or civil strife. Public quiet."

In turn, Dawn, Christopher, Iris, and Derrick shouted as loudly as they could:

"Calm!"

"Quiet!"

"Tranquility!"

"Serenity!"

When the laughter ebbed, Alec stated simply, "Peace: 'That which passeth all our understanding.'"

"Yes, Alec, that is a very fine definition." Zac wrote *PEACE* on the board with white chalk and below the word drew the familiar insignia. "I think that concludes 'Words We Should Know' for today. It's time for simple mathematics. Iris, you may begin by defining a ton."

"Did you want the long ton or the short ton?" Iris smirked.

"Under the circumstances, Iris, the short ton. Yes, under these particular circumstances the short ton, which is used in the United States and other parts of the world, will do very nicely. Do let us have the short ton."

"Nine hundred and seven point twenty kilograms or two thousand pounds avoirdupois," she answered, drawling out the French absurdly.

"Exactly right, Iris, very good. Very good, indeed. Now for an easy one, one we've had before. We'll give it to Christo because he's youngest. Ready?"

Christopher nodded nervously.

"What is a megaton?"

"One million tons!" crowed Christopher.

"And how many tons in twenty megatons, Christo?"

"Twenty million tons!" Christopher looked to Dawn for praise. She smiled with maternal pride.

"Excellent," said Zac. "Now for a more difficult problem. One requiring computation. Derrick, we'll leave it to you."

Derrick swaggered to the blackboard.

"All right, old man, assume that the population of greater London is approximately eight million persons."

8,000,000 wrote Derrick with red chalk.

"Assume a disaster in which seventy-five percent of that population is destroyed. How many are the number of the dead?"

Derrick muttered as he wrote. "Seventy-five percent equals three fourths. Four goes into eight twice. One fourth equals two million dead persons. If one fourth equals two million, then three fourths equals three times . . ."

"Six million dead persons," Alec called.

"All right, Mr. Smarter." Derrick turned and threw the chalk at him. "I'm the one who's to do it, not you." Picking up fresh chalk, he concluded lamely, "Six million dead persons."

"That, I think, covers simple mathematics for today."

"This is your early warning system," blared the tape recorder. "Blue alert! Blue alert! Prepare to take shelter. This is not a test. We repeat, this is not a test."

"We'll just have time for our last lesson. You will answer in chorus, please," Zac said quietly.

> "While dear old Rome was burning
> What was the emperor doing,
> Day and night, night and day?"

> "Fiddling away, fiddling away."

Madsong

"In Auschwitz the ovens were burning
Day and night, night and day."

"People stuffed their noses with roses,
They looked the other way."

"When Nagasaki was burning,
What did they do in New York?"

"They popped a champagne cork."

"And what are they doing in Windsor,
While bombs are falling in Asia,
Day and night, night and day?"

"Oh Windsor people are gay.
Asia is so far away.
Yes, Windsor people are gay."

"Red alert! Red alert! Take shelter at once!"
The siren pierced the air and then there was a deafening explosion. On the screen the mushroom cloud unfolded in slow motion like an opening flower.

The set grew dark except for one pool of light illuminating Anna and the panda on the floor by her desk. She shuddered, writhed, stiffened, went limp. She stretched her hand out beseechingly to the panda. The light went out.

After a moment's silence, the image of Christopher wandered onto the screen. Shuffling slowly, he walked the length of a deserted field. His small figure finally disappeared beyond camera range.

The play was over, the lights came up.

"How I loathe messages!" the buxom matron exclaimed. "There's no such thing as entertainment these days. It's all messages and perversion. The children were charming, of course, but how very depressing it was. I'd much rather a good laugh or a good cry, really I would."

"I thought that schoolmaster chap did a marvelous job of direction," the young man said.

"I'm sure you're right, darling; I just wish it had been a bit more cheerful. I had poor Vickie the better part of the afternoon, please remember," she replied as he maneuvered her out of the room.

"Foolish woman," Lew whispered harshly to Joy.

Zac bore down upon them.

"What did you think, Joy? I must have your candid reaction. Wasn't it splendid? Wasn't Alec superb? His face had them howling. And Iris's wondrous titter—it's perfect; mere art could not improve upon it. Did you notice my stroke of genius? We did 'God Save the Queen' first so as not to diminish the ending. And the rhymes, Joy . . . You put me on to them. Anna's death doesn't please me though. There's more to be done there. Come now, you haven't told me what you think."

"You haven't given me the chance. I think it's an interesting experiment and parts of it are effective. You're right about Anna, however, and I have my doubts about the ending as well—Christopher, all alone, tramping the great empty field. It's what we call schmaltz . . . a little too sentimental, perhaps."

"That scene was, in fact, Lew's idea," Zac explained with some embarrassment.

"The ending is not sentimental," Lew snapped. "It

simply makes painfully clear the consequences of inaction by engaging the audience with the fate of one little boy."

"Oh, for God's sake," Joy protested.

"Quiet you two," laughed Zac. "There'll be no jousting on this night of triumph."

At the hotel Zac stopped in the lounge for a pint of celebration with Lew, while Joy accompanied the children to their rooms.

"Did you really and truly like the play?" Iris breathlessly inquired at five-minute intervals.

"I thought you were all splendid, every last one of you," Joy persistently replied and even Derrick warmed to her praise.

"Didn't I ever give it old Alec!" he chortled, throwing a rare companionable arm across Alec's shoulders.

"Yes, you most certainly did, and Alec took it like a man," she said. The pleasure in Alec's eyes, occasioned by Derrick's unexpected gesture, was painful to see. "Comedy is the most difficult thing in the world, but Alec's got a gift for it."

Proving her point, Alec threw himself on a bed, as if prostrated by her praise.

"Alec's an old idiot, that's what Alec is," sneered Derrick, signaling an end to their truce.

When the others were settled down, Joy paid a visit to Anna. The child seemed unnaturally silent and withdrawn amid the excitement of the others. It was clear that Anna was by nature a brooder; nevertheless, her behavior was disquieting.

She was propped on an elbow, reading to the panda, her face screwed up with astigmatic concentration in spite of her glasses. She broke off in the middle of a sentence as Joy sat down on the edge of the bed.

"The Grimms are a little grim, don't you think, Anna? I always found their stories depressing. He might have nightmares," she said, although the implacable stare of the panda suggested that his dream life was not a problem.

"He likes them very much. We've done *The Golden Bird, Hans in Luck,* and *The Frog Prince.*"

"*The Frog Prince* is one I know well. 'For long have you lain, in trouble and pain, like a frog in a well, fast bound by a spell.' As I recall, that one has a happily-ever-after."

"Yes," said Anna, "we thought the ending very nice. Now we're doing *The Straw, the Coal, and the Bean.*"

"Reading to a stupid bear. Did you ever hear anything so ridiculous?" called Iris from the other side of the room.

Joy thought feverishly and finally countered, "I think you're wrong there, Iris. Reading aloud is fast becoming a lost art. Its passing is to be regretted. It used to be a family habit. Everyone gathered in the drawing room of an evening and shared a story."

"I'm sure there weren't any bears in the drawing room." Iris pulled her blankets over her ears.

"If you're going to read, Anna, I wish you'd get on with it," said Dawn sleepily. "You left off in the middle of a sentence."

"Yes, do go on, Anna. If you don't mind, I'll just sit here and listen. I haven't heard a fairy tale in a long time."

Anna synopsized. "You see, there's this old woman who's making beans in a great pot, but one bean gets away and goes and makes friends with a straw and a coal who have also escaped from the old woman."

Muffled noises of annoyance came from Iris's bed.

Anna cleared her throat dramatically.

"The Coal answered: 'I have happily escaped the fire; and if I had not done so by force of will, my death would certainly have been a most cruel one; I should have been burnt to a cinder.'

'My opinion is,' said the Bean, 'that, as we have escaped death, we must all keep together like good comrades; and so that we may run no further risks, we had better quit the country.'

I think I'll stop now and leave the rest for tomorrow. He likes suspense," Anna confided, looking down at the panda.

"That's a very good idea, my dear. It's time for both of you to be sleeping."

"Zac isn't pleased with my dying, is he, Joy? Do you think he'll give the part to someone else?"

"You're not to worry about that, Anna. Zac wasn't really displeased. He just wants to make it better. Dying takes practice, I suspect. If someone were to ask me to die, I wouldn't know where to begin. Just between us, I thought you did it beautifully."

"Truly?"

"Truly. I was convinced utterly." Joy removed the

steel-rimmed glasses from Anna's worried face. "Tell me, Anna, you do know what a play is, don't you?"

"Yes, a play's just pretend."

"That's right, just a lot of silly pretend. Time to close your eyes. My, what a long day it's been. Sleep now."

Anna twined her legs connubially around the panda and Joy drew the covers over her.

"Not asleep, are you?" whispered Zac.

"No. I didn't know if you would come."

"I've just dispatched the Llewelyn—sent him staggering back to London. After two pints, Lew's a roarer. You should have come down and joined us. You missed the fun. After just two pints, Lew becomes a complete someone else. You'd like the someone else, better than you like Lew, I'm sure. Are the children tucked away?"

"Next you'll be asking did I put the cat out and wind the clock."

"No, that isn't at all what I came in to ask. We'll leave the clock unwound."

"You called out for someone."

"Yes, I know. Please forgive me, Zac."

"There's no need for forgiveness. Was he someone you loved?"

"Yes. He's dead now."

"You were with him?"

"Yes."

"And it was good?"

"When it was good, it was very, very good, and when it was bad . . . so it goes. Do you know what we are,

Zac? We're good comrades, keeping together, who have quit the country."

"You'll have to explain that one to me."

"It's just some nonsense from a fairy tale Anna was reading, improbably entitled *The Straw, the Coal, and the Bean*."

"The cast does not sound propitious, but I want you to have the feeling that you've run away with me and we're making our own country—a place without time."

"Speaking of Anna, Zac . . ."

"Were we?"

"I want to. Are you sure all this dying is good for her? She seemed very moody tonight."

"That's just Anna's way. She loves dying."

"Exactly my point. It's morbid. And another thing . . . What about this foundation of Llewelyn's? It sounds very strange. How on earth have you explained to it my being here?"

"In the first place, you're not to fret about Anna; in the second place, you're not to fret about the foundation. I dislike women who fret. As I've said before, it's the play that's important. The foundation simply pays the bills. It's financed and, in the main, run by a collection of rich old pussies, the kind that suspect nefarious doings up at the vicarage. The foundation keeps their minds off local mischief. If they had any idea of some of the things that are in the play, they'd have me publicly hanged and posthumously dismembered. So far we've been in luck, been able to keep the matter dark."

"But Lew intimated this evening that the foundation was far to the left of Labour."

"Sometimes Lew is an absolute ass. That's just his wishful thinking. There are a few younger hangers-on, like Lew, in need of changing the world and hoping to leech onto the foundation, but they hardly get anywhere. The old pussies will not be moved. The play's the only exception I know of. So please stop fretting. Not to worry, love."

" 'Don't worry, darling' . . . 'There's nothing to worry about, dear' . . . 'not to worry, love.' Love songs of the western world."

When her breathing was finally deep and regular, Zac left quietly and switched on the light in his own room. It was 2:45 . . . two hours of working time and he'd still get three hours of sleep to see him through the day. Sitting down at the desk, he contemplated.

The basement flat had but one window.

He hoped to focus the story upon the deterioration of the relationship between the two characters as a result of the mounting political tension during those awful days in the fall of '38. In the final scene, with England's capitulation an accomplished fact, the Czech girl, helpless and confused, would seek comfort, but the Englishman would be rendered impotent—thus history, reenacted in the bed.

The irony of his project was not lost on Zac. If his play was propaganda for peace, then his story would have as its background the dangers of appeasement. He smiled to himself.

Joy had already given him the name of his hero—he would call his character Stephen—and, of course, she had also given him the first love scene. It only remained to name the heroine. Helena, Zac decided. Although it was hardly Slavic, it was certainly euphonious.

Closing his eyes, Zac visualized the basement flat in every detail. Finally he began to write.

An hour later he read over the first love scene critically. It was no good, he decided. He was facing the age-old problem. It was almost impossible to write about sex without reducing it to gymnastics or mechanics.

Zac stretched and yawned, thinking that with war and love, love and war, it had been a very long day.

Joy stirred in her sleep, threw one arm across the bed, sensed Zac's absence, and awoke. Her room was unbearably cold. She lit the electric heater and considered the possibility of early tea. Because her watch was broken, she was unsure of the time and afraid it was too early to call for some. She went to the window. The first dull rays of the cold dawn outlined the Garter Tower. Drawing a chair close to the heater, she opened the long-ledger for the first time since Stephen's death and wrote idly.

> *His hands and mouth sought*
> *Their path upon me,*
> *Found their way*
> *In rhythm and in fire . . .*

She slammed the book shut. Women wrote a lot of nonsense about sex, invariably calling it love; whereas, men wrote a lot of nonsense about love, invariably calling it sex. Both men and women were far too humorless on the subject.

Zac's humor delighted her. Like Stephen he could take flight in a spinning rush of words from the least quotidian . . .

She drowsed . . . half asleep . . . suddenly adream . . .

On the high wire Stephen danced with danger—the original acrobat with no equilibrium, without the ground sense of gravity. At a lower level Zac tightroped with an orange umbrella. Watching them both quizzically, arms folded, legs apart, Rolf straddled solid earth.

Joy awoke with a start and huddled closer to the warmth coming from the glowing coils.

Child's Play, Act Two

It was their first morning in Cambridge and the first day of sun in nearly a week. Joy woke late from a good sleep and remembered happily that the morning before her was a morning to herself. Zac had packed himself and the brood off to an early rehearsal.

The luxury of the Royal Cambridge Hotel almost compensated for their three horrible days in Oxford. There the foundation had booked them into what was without doubt the most decrepit rooming house in the city. The woman who ran it, an incarnation of the wicked witch, refused to provide more than one towel for each child during their stay, and breakfast consisted chiefly of grease. The gas meters in two of their four rooms didn't work, and the window of the bathroom shared by the eight of them was broken. The antagonism between Derrick and Alec, irritated by the discomfort of the situation, finally erupted into violence. Backed into a corner by Derrick, Alec defended himself with unsuccessful vigor. The results: a torrential nosebleed, an emergency trip to the local clinic, and a five-pound note to cover the cost of cleaning one of the witch's rugs.

Joy was now fully reassured as to the harmless nature of the foundation, for she had actually met one of the old pussies. Mrs. Fitzwilliams-Smith, complete with cameo brooch and an encyclopedic knowledge of the genealogy of the Christian saints, appeared briefly after the second performance of the play in Oxford. However, Joy was still worried about the effect of the play on Anna. The child grew daily more morose, despite Zac's protestations to the contrary. He was forever closeting himself with Anna in the name of rehearsal, and whenever he did so, Joy felt there was something sinister about it, something she didn't understand but didn't care to think about, for in just a few days she had become attached to Zac.

Zac took her out of herself, made her laugh, and he seemed to delight in doing it. Even during the worst moments in Oxford, with Alec spouting blood like a small injured whale and the witch screeching about her rug, Zac made her laugh.

Joy dressed slowly, then wandered into his room. His clothes were strewn about, and the desk was littered with scrawled sheets of paper, some bearing the arms of the Windsor hotel, some the more florid decoration of the Royal Cambridge. Joy began to decipher the story—for what was written in the form of fiction was surely meant to be read.

The story began on the day Hitler delivered his ultimatum demanding the Czechoslovakian territory. Zac described London's terror of imminent war and eventual invasion and the city's drastic defense preparations: the sudden appearance everywhere of trenches, batteries, and searchlights. Joy thought that the translation of the world from normality into fear was done very well.

Zac's two characters lived in a small apartment in the middle of the city. For the Englishman, Zac had appropriated Stephen's name. The girl, Helena, was a Czech. Whereas the Londoners feared war, Helena feared—prophetically—that there would be no war, that ultimately her country would be sacrificed. Although she loved him, Helena blamed Stephen for the hesitancy—she called it cowardice—of his country.

Believably female, Joy thought.

So far the story consisted largely of wireless broadcasts the two characters listened to, their desultory conversation, which became more nervous and more angry as greater and greater political tension was reported, and some rather desperate lovemaking. Joy was appalled by the love scene. There was no invention at all in it. Zac had used her for copy and merely reported—too clinically—what went on between them.

Zac was a thief of words as well as acts. At the conclusion of the scene the character Helena, momentarily at peace, recited: "We're good comrades, keeping together, who have quit the country."

"What an absurd thing to have said," Joy muttered aloud. Zac needed to learn that when art too closely imitated life, the inevitable result was banality.

So much for fairy tales.

Determined to ignore his nonsense, Joy left the hotel and headed up Trumpington Street toward the center of Cambridge in search of someone to repair her watch. She had gone on too long without knowing the time. If the rest of the world kept time, it was necessary to keep time with it.

She found a shop specializing in old china which also advertised—in decorous small print as if the activity were onerous—the repair of watches. The proprietor was courteous but adamant. Her watch was doomed, he said, at least for as long as she remained abroad. There wasn't a man in the kingdom that could be expected to do a thing with it.

Joy purchased an inexpensive pocket watch and slipped it into her purse. As she was about to leave the shop, a stack of dinner plates caught her attention. They were early Staffordshire and brightly colored. They pictured a marvelously haughty peacock on the verge of preening and announcing to the world that he wouldn't preen until he was damn ready. She considered buying the plates . . . a wedding gift for her father, perhaps, should he win as well as woo the widow. They would match the house perfectly. She remembered the proverbs in her father's study . . . *The pride of the peacock is the glory of God* . . . and inquired about the price. It was prohibitive.

Ignoring the proprietor, who hovered discreetly but expectantly in the background, she ran her fingers over the surface of the top plate, lingering with the form of the arrogant peacock. Although it had endured more than a century of catastrophe, the plate was still intact. There were faint veins of damage invading the porcelain, but it was still whole.

"They are lovely, are they not?" the proprietor asked encouragingly. "So elegant and yet done with such imagination. They are truly unique."

"Yes, they are truly unique," Joy agreed and left the shop.

She wandered through the grounds of several colleges, visited the Cam, and by midafternoon her annoyance with Zac was gone. If he had used her as copy, it was perhaps no real treachery. Words were his work, and a man's vision of the acts of love was always different from a woman's. Zac was good to her. No doubt she ought to be flattered to be a part of his story.

"So much sophistry," muttered Cousin Patricia, crossing the small bridge from one bank of the river to the other, appropriately dressed for a cold day's punting.

Joy reconsidered Zac's story. She didn't particularly care for it, but she thought she understood what he was trying to get at . . . the fluid, formless, essentially ineffectual private lives people led when the public mood was one of uneasiness and waiting. Seepage, again. But, after all, one didn't have to go all the way to 1938, all the way to Munich for that.

Joy had promised to meet Zac and the children at their rehearsal, and with the help of the pocket watch she arrived on time. A large, stark room had been reserved for the play's use, and the children and Zac were hard at it. In the center of the room Zac knelt beside Anna, crouched on the floor. Anna listened to Zac's hypnotic whispering while the other children kept absolutely still.

"Now, Anna, I want you to make everything blank. You're not here, Anna, and I'm not here. You're in the middle of an empty circle. Do you see the empty circle, Anna? Do you feel it?"

"Yes, Zac."

"Good. Let us fill the empty circle. Think now of a smell. Think how the classroom smells. Chalk dust, disinfectant, the polish they use on the desks . . . and now the sounds . . ."

Anna spoke. "I hear Christopher scratching his pen on the paper. He always makes a horrid noise, and Iris is shuffling her shoes back and forth . . ."

"Good, Anna, good. Let us fill the empty circle with more things. The siren has just blown three times and you're very frightened. You've got down on the floor, and now you are alone in a very dark place . . . there is no one, no one. You can't see. The noise comes, louder than the worst thunder; it explodes, inside your head, inside your body, and now you can't hear, Anna. You're alone in a very dark place; you can't see, Anna; you can't hear, Anna; you can't feel, Anna . . . and now . . . there is no Anna."

With a gesture of caution to the other children, Zac moved quietly away from Anna.

She twisted herself into a rigid ball, hands over her ears, eyes squeezed shut. She looked like a frozen homunculus. Her unearthly shriek shattered the silence and her little body convulsed once and then lay completely still for what seemed an unnaturally long time.

Just as Joy was about to rush to her, Anna came out of it, rubbing her eyes, looking around uncertainly.

"Bravo! Lovely, Anna, lovely. Far better than I ever dreamed it could be!" Zac applauded with awe in his voice.

Anna responded with a radiant smile, but Joy still was disturbed by the look of the child. She seemed confused and half asleep. However, she knew Zac didn't like her to interfere, so she said nothing, but smiled reassuringly as Anna, having retrieved her panda from a corner of the room, exclaimed, "Did you hear? Zac says it's going to be fine!"

"There you are, Joy . . ." Zac came toward her. "Wasn't Anna superb? What a day we've had. I went off in a rush this morning, quite forgetting my tie, and would you believe that that officious bastard of a head-waiter at the hotel barred me from breakfast? On this day of all days, when who should be breakfasting in that very dining room but a venerable English novelist. I sent the children on in by themselves and dashed back to my room for the tie because the man of letters was nearly through his kipper. By the time I returned, he had departed. Because of the idiocy of custom, I was denied all but a brief glimpse of him. He has the face of a very ancient, very wise, very amiable mouse. How I should have liked a talk with such a mouse, but it was not to be. We came on here first thing after breakfast to find the place packed with oddments of furniture. We had to sniff out and hound someone in authority to get the stuff moved. Finally the room was cleared, everything was arranged, we began—began poorly, got worse. It's only in the last hour that things have begun to tick smoothly. Luckily you came in on Anna's triumph and missed the rest."

"Speaking of ticking, I've a new watch." She took it from her purse and displayed it.

"I rather liked you without time."

"I say, that's a handsome watch," Alec said heartily.

"It looks perfectly ordinary to me," scoffed Derrick. "My father has a watch that tells not just the hour and minute, but the day, the month, the year, and the position of the heavenly bodies as well." As if mere description could not do such a watch justice, Derrick added, "My father has the best watch in the universe."

"Anna, what do you think of my new watch?" Joy held the watch to the panda's ear.

Anna looked at her blankly and did not answer.

"Naps, naps for us all! But a nap first and foremost for old Zac, for he's a weary man."

Joy knew he was trying to distract her from Anna.

When they reached the hotel, Zac insisted that the children keep to their rooms for awhile. Joy left them more or less reconciled to his command. Anna, seemingly recovered, was reading to the panda, and Dawn and Christopher provided her with a secondary audience. While Iris watched, Alec and Derrick dealt out one of their interminable games of War. They played it offstage as well as on.

Zac ordered tea and as she poured he asked, "What made you buy the watch?"

"I just felt the need of one and couldn't get my old one fixed. I can't go on in limbo for the rest of my life not knowing the time."

"I think there's more to it. I thought we were going to forget about time for a bit."

"Perhaps you're right. I was in your room this morning and read your story. It was lying out on the desk."

"Good. I've been debating with myself whether or not to have you read it before it was truly finished. What did you think of it? It has its moments, don't you agree? I think the description of London digging in for invasion awfully good. I was surprised how clearly I remembered it. I was only five at the time of the Crisis. And the basic idea of the story—that seems to me to be sound."

"I'm not sure I can judge your story objectively," she said dryly. "I seem to be in it."

"Yes, yes. There's something about you I'm trying to capture, something that moves me. A feeling of solitariness, perhaps. I want the reader to feel it about Helena. Very difficult to do, very difficult." He sipped his tea.

"Zac, you're beyond belief! Hasn't it occurred to you that I might find it unnerving to *read* our lovemaking, that I might feel you've used me?"

"Why on earth should you? Helena is a beautiful character."

"Can't you see her beauty isn't the point? The point is the privacy of our relationship."

"Privacy!" Zac pronounced the word with incredulity and in the British way, bringing to Joy's mind a very clear picture of Selma's outhouse. "How exactly like a woman.

Now, love, you are to put away this nonsense immediately. I simply won't have it."

Although her close knowledge of the play made her hypercritical, Joy thought the Cambridge performance was the best yet. The audience was responsive, and so far the technical details—tape, film, and lighting—had gone off without a hitch. The children acted with spontaneity regardless of the rehearsing Zac had forced upon them.

"Red alert! Red alert! Take shelter at once!"

The siren.

The faces of the audience froze. Most of them knew what to expect. They had been there before. Joy realized that Zac must have been a child about Anna's age during the worst of the Second World War.

The explosion. The mushroom cloud—with all its exquisite symmetry—in slow motion.

Anna shrieked, twisted in agony, died.

Christopher trudged across the screen, disappeared.

A small circle of light still held Anna. Her gaze was as blank as that of the eyeless panda. The unnatural silence went on.

"Anna! Oh, my God!"

Anna did not move.

Anna began to come around, Zac rushed her off to a hospital, and Joy shepherded the other children back to the hotel. They were dazed and docile: Alec's face registered adult compassion; Dawn and Christopher clung together, a double image of innocent confusion; and even Iris and Derrick seemed remarkably subdued.

"It was those terrible stories," murmured Alec.

Joy glanced at the battered copy of *Grimm's Tales* on Anna's bed. "No, Alec," she soothed, "it has nothing to do with the fairy stories. It's just that Anna's tired and needs to rest. She'll be all right tomorrow . . ."

"He's not talking about *those* stories," Derrick interrupted.

The children waited for her reaction.

"What stories are you talking about, Alec?"

Alec appealed silently to Derrick.

"Just stories that Zac tells sometimes while we're rehearsing," Derrick explained with forced casualness.

The children busied themselves with preparations for bed.

"Now just one minute," Joy protested. "I want to know what this is all about. What kind of stories has Zac been telling?"

"About the war," Derrick replied shortly.

"What it was like when he was a boy in the war," Alec elaborated.

"Terrible stories," said Dawn with a shiver.

"Oh, it's just Anna," Iris said scornfully. "She's such a big silly. The least little thing frightens her."

"Once upon a time, a long time ago, when he was a very little boy, the bombs came, and Zac was buried in a cellar. He was all by himself . . . all alone. Yes, he was. And there were spiders and rats, and he couldn't breathe, and then some men came and got him out. And Zac is always telling Anna about it." Having unburdened himself, Christopher shrunk back into Dawn's motherly embrace.

"That was once upon a very long time ago indeed," Joy said by way of feeble reassurance. The children turned away from her and, too quietly, continued to get ready for bed.

For the first time the children presented a united front, and Joy sensed condemnation, or at least mistrust, of herself as well as Zac in their attitude. It was no wonder, she thought, returning to her own room. She had ignored the insistent promptings which told her that there was something wrong with Anna. Her indifference was partly to blame. Zac, however, could not be fathomed. He was not indifferent. He was fond of the children— his brood. She was sure his affection was sincere, and yet he deliberately terrorized an eight-year-old child for a purpose as trivial as that hodgepodge of platitudes, politics, and bathos he called a play. It was impossible to believe that Zac was a sadist, but it was almost equally difficult to believe that he was fool enough to confuse his amateur production with an altar of art requiring a sacrificial lamb—a lamb nearsighted and already neurotic.

Zac burst into the room.

"Not a word, Joy, because I know exactly what you're going to say. You were right. I admit it. So let's have an end to it before it begins. You see, no harm's been done. Anna rests easy, all tucked in with panda. She's a perfectly normal Anna now, and tomorrow morning we can fetch her. When we perform in London, I shall simply turn over the dying to one of the others. Iris, perhaps. Her skin's as thick as an armadillo's. Anna shall never die again. I do promise, Joy, really I do. It's a pity though.

Anna was so convincing . . . Oh, I'm a weary man." He
came toward her.
"Keep away from me, Zac. Don't touch me."

Zac sat at the desk whispering to himself.
"Zac, old man, will you never learn? The ways of a
woman are like the ways of the Lord, strange and mys-
terious, and to the merely mortal mind, inscrutable."
Still, the recent unpleasantness with Joy had put him
in precisely the right mood to get on with his story.
Fingertips pressed to his temples, he prepared for a
frontal attack on the final scene. It would begin with
Chamberlain's voice over the wireless declaring that war
had been averted, Czechoslovakia had been sacrificed.
Stephen would find himself unable to comfort Helena
and, finally, incapable of making love to her. Zac felt he
was just weary enough to enter into the experience fully.
It went well. An hour and a half later he wrote out the
last sentence:
He was much too tired to think things through. De-
cisions were for tomorrow.
Zac stretched himself out as far as he could in his chair,
enjoying the cramp in his neck and the ache in his back
as signs of a day well spent.

Joy was curled in the armchair in her father's study with
a comforter over her. Part of a proverb was illuminated:
The hours of folly are measur'd by the clock . . .

Finale

The following week the world caught up with Zac. Mrs. Fitzwilliams-Smith of the cameo brooch informed the foundation of old pussies that the play was not simply Christian ethics out of the mouths of babes. It was also discovered that Zac had been traveling, under their auspices, with a woman who was not his wife. The play would not be performed again. Llewelyn abjured the foundation, claiming that there was nothing in all the world but the vast meow of Christian pussies.

Anna recovered, but her parents, enraged because Zac had temporarily disrupted the delicate equipoise of her nature, threatened to sue.

Zac submitted his story through a friend of a friend to a magazine and was promised a quick decision.

Joy was aware of these events but only from a distance. After returning to London, she met Zac only once—for a short, perfunctory farewell.

Zac entered his favorite local and signaled for the drawing of a pint of his usual. Lew was already there, waiting for him. Lew was always early, but today his eager smile was particularly welcome.

"What an afternoon I've had!"

"What happened, Zac? Are they going to print it?"

"I got in to see the chief chap, the ruddy arbiter of taste himself. Much good it did me. He won't take, doesn't like. He says the story's dated. The Second World War's passé; everyone finds it a bore. As for love affairs, if he is to be believed, no one has had one since the thirties. In a word, they are irrelevant. He says short fiction has got to be mod or mad. Or spies. Spies are very timely. Mod spies in a mad world, or mad spies in a mod world: those are the alternatives. These days nothing else will do. I asked him if all British fiction must be degenerate. He didn't have an answer to that, you may be sure. Drink up now—there's a good, a very stout lad. Time for another and another and another . . ."

The evening lengthened, lubricated by the publican's best draught. Lew provided an audience of one—willing and warm.

"The thing of it is not to let it get me down. I'll just keep sending the story round . . . sooner or later . . ."

"That's right, Zac, exactly right. Don't let it get you down. It's a bloody good story!" Lew thumped Zac on the back. He had reached the threshold of roaring. "My round. We'll drink to a bloody good story!" He walked toward the bar and disappeared in the crowd.

Zac awaited Lew's return uneasily. The play was gone

the brood was gone, Joy was gone . . . and now the story . . .

The crowd expanded, the walls contracted while Zac waited. Sometimes it happened in the tube or a lift. Slow panic, suffocation, a jangling in his head which became louder and louder until he was a child, back in the cellar with the creatures he could hear but not see, which attacked unless he kept awake, flailing his arms and legs.

Zac bolted—crashing his way through the crowd and into the street. He gasped in fresh air until his head cleared.

"Zac, are you all right?" Lew called from the doorway of the pub.

"Just a little tight, Lew. Need a walk." He waved and walked on down the street. As he turned the corner, he saw Lew following several paces behind.

Catching up. Lew explained diffidently, "I just thought you might need some help."

Zac smiled. "Good old Lew," he said, flinging an arm around Lew's shoulders. "Good man."

The dormitory lights were turned off, bringing Anna's evening reading to an end before she had reached the conclusion of the story of Iron Hans, who was bewitched and changed into a Wild Man.

With her hand covering the panda's ears, she whispered to him: "We're alone in a very dark place, and there is no one, and we can't see, and we can't hear, and we can't feel . . ."

Over Ireland, Joy thought regretfully about Zac and seepage.

Wrapped in Harris tweed topped by London Fog, Cousin Patricia unreeled a sardonic series of epithets: "Two-bit Svengali, Method Director, Votary of Art . . ."

Over the Atlantic, Joy leafed through a month of magazines. Because of the flu and the trip, she was sadly out of touch. The color photographs of the moon's surface, of the earth in the distance, were superb, and the President's Inaugural Ball obviously had been a very well-dressed affair.

Over Newfoundland, she slept.

THREE

GOLDEN GATE

Decline and Fall

In eight months Cousin Patricia had undergone a rather disastrous transformation. For one thing, she was younger; for another, she was careless in the matters of dress and speech. Wearing a short skirt and a long sweater of indeterminate character and origin, she did not grace the aisles of I. Magnin. Joy, in pearl-grey cashmere, did, as she surveyed the gift silver displayed on the mezzanine.

"Why don't you settle for a case of Geritol?" Patricia asked with a dig-in-the-ribs laugh. "That's what the old boy is going to need."

Although her father was to marry the widow in December, at the semester's end, and the widow looked like a lively one, Joy still found their embrace beyond conceiving.

She gave up the idea of silver. Under the circumstances

it was too ordinary a gift. The peacock plates, presumably still sitting in the Cambridge shop, were to be regretted. Now she could easily afford them.

She left Magnin's, bought the *Chronicle*, and read the headlines.

Two Sharp Jolts
QUAKES HIT BAY AREA

The previous evening the strongest earthquakes in eight years had hit San Francisco, registering 5.6 on the Richter scale. Buildings shook and windows were broken, but at the opera the third act of *La Boheme* was not interrupted, and no one deserted the Top of the Mark.

Today all was normal again. It was the second day of October, and the city was enjoying the last spell of fine weather before the rainy season. At a corner stall Joy bought yellow roses (moist, not yet open, but promising a rich fragrance) and hailed a cab. Golden Gate Park was on her way.

Coals to Newcastle, she thought, as she left the cab and, with the roses in her arms, wandered through a maze of flower beds to the heart of the park.

She and Rolf spent several hours every Sunday in the park, and Joy often visited it during the week. Conservatory, museum, aquarium, planetarium. They felt that the park was the universe encapsulated for their benefit—and what a show it was.

She checked the planetarium's coming events and decided to forego *Five Ways to Doomsday* but not to miss *Birth of Our Solar System*. In the tea garden she had jasmine tea, strolled for a half hour among the shrines and miniature gardens, then checked her watch. It was an Omega with a snaky gold band—Rolf's wedding present to her—and she was still unused to seeing it on her wrist.

She was expected in the early afternoon, and she set out to walk the short distance.

Selma lived in a plummeting but lively neighborhood: one part students to two parts minorities. Things had not gone well with her. Mr. Quick was dead, killed by a runaway car on one of the hills, and Selma blamed herself for letting him run at night in spite of city ordinances. The night after his death she went off . . . down to the devils with a very resounding whump. The police found her toward dawn, derailed and raging on Fisherman's Wharf. She had been robbed and slapped around a little by a group of marauding teenagers. She couldn't remember too much about it, she said. After that: downhill all the way. She developed obscure eye trouble, as yet undiagnosed by her doctor. Joy kept trying to get her to a specialist, but Selma had either an aversion to or a superstition about specialists. She could not really stray beyond the immediate neighborhood in safety, and she would not be persuaded to get another dog. The students on the street liked her, kept an eye on her, and lent a hand when she would let them. Joy stopped by in the early afternoon two or three times a week.

Joy closed herself and flowers into the two-person, self-service, upward-bound coffin and prayed. The elevator launched itself and lurched to the proper floor. She let herself into Selma's apartment.

In one corner of the living room, a small scented can-dle burned: Mr. Quick's eternal flame—and a shrine to other dead things, Joy suspected. As always the TV played softly. An elegant roué whispered suavely, "Why don't we leave the problem of Stephanie to Vanessa."

For some reason NET did not come in very clearly in the city, and Selma was reduced to the "soapies" until early evening.

Selma was crouched over in a chair, a magnifying glass in one hand and a large type copy of *Time* in the other. A standing, two-armed lamp trained 300 watts of light on the page.

"Oh, how you smell!" Selma's voice was the same—in perpetual need of clearing.

Joy turned off the TV and brought the roses over.

"Hmmm . . ." Selma inhaled the flowers. "I keep telling you you don't have to . . ."

Without waiting for the end of the sentence, Joy took the flowers into the kitchen and filled an empty milk bottle with water for them. "Beer, Selma?" she called.

"I might."

Pleased, Joy took two cans from the refrigerator. Lately Selma's intake was much diminished, and so was her spirit.

"What about those quakes last night? Weren't they out of sight? Didn't they just blow your mind?" Since the neighborhood students had discovered and cared for her, Selma took pride in proving herself hip in one sentence out of every fifty.

Joy delivered beer and flowers to the table next to Selma's chair and sensed that Selma was on the edge of a major disclosure.

Decline and Fall

"Well, I've got another earthquake for you! Haven't seen this, have you?" Selma flourished *Time.*

"No. What's new?"

"Stevie. Stevie's famous. Stevie's in *Time.*"

Shocked to hear the name—Selma was usually overly careful not to mention it—Joy took the magazine and read the article in the art section incredulously.

Stephen's work had been discovered, was hung in a gallery, had a small cult of followers. Apparently he was particularly popular with the young because of his treatment of violence. He saw violence as a natural force, a beautiful force, a force with which the individual could join in ecstatic communion. There followed two pages of colored photographs of the peak paintings. The article went on to say that at heart Stephen was a Neoplatonist.

Caught with her intellectual pants down, Joy rushed to Selma's dictionary, ensconced between *Sloth* and *Lust.*

neoplatonism n, usu cap : a philosophical school originating in Alexandria, modifying the teachings of Plato to accord with Aristotelian, post-Aristotelian, and oriental conceptions and conceiving of the world as an emanation from the One with whom the soul is capable of being reunited in trance or ecstasy.

neoplatonist n, usu cap : an advocate of Neoplatonism.

Joy still didn't understand. Could flesh be Neoplatonic, could heart? An interview with Stephen's father was even more implausible. He claimed that Stephen was very religious and lived among the mountains like a monk on a retreat. He claimed that Stephen lost his life climbing a mountain to get closer to God.

"How absurd."

"Well, I always say you never know, you just never know."

"Nonsense. I do know. He walked up that damned mountain because he was out of his head and then he didn't have the sense to go in out of the snow. Like a child, a stupid child. Whenever I think about it, I get so angry . . ."

"Now, now, sweetie . . ."

"It's true. Anger is the thing I feel most about him. He had no right to die."

"It was his transaction." Selma sighed enigmatically.

"What does that mean?"

"We've got to write Max about it right now." Selma changed the subject decisively.

Max was in Miami, in the used-car business, having failed as a ladies' shoe salesman in Sante Fe. (According to Max, the hook put the ladies off.) He wrote Selma every week, asking when she was going to come on down; the weather was fine and, after all, they weren't getting any younger. No, Selma said, no; what did Max need with an old, half-blind ruin? But Joy was of the opinion that Selma would finally weaken and consent.

Selma dictated with exaggerated slowness: "Dear Maxus, guess what? Our Stevie is famous."

"Max didn't like Stephen toward the end," Joy commented, recording Selma's words with a blunt pencil on a yellow pad.

Selma was not deterred. She dictated a page and a half. Joy added her own affectionate greetings and went to a drawer to rummage for an envelope and a stamp.

When she turned back, Selma's face was twisted, her body rigid. She stared in the direction of Mr. Quick's shrine and blinked back tears.

"The devils?" Joy asked softly, crossing the room.

Selma nodded.

They came with greater and greater frequency and often without a cause. Now, there seemed to be no day when she was entirely free from visitation.

Joy slipped down to the floor, put her arms on Selma's knees, and laid her head in her arms to wait for Selma to dispel the devils. Selma curled a strand of Joy's hair around her finger and struggled for exorcism.

After long minutes of trying to invent something to amuse, Joy looked up. "Do you know what I'm going to do . . . ?" She paused to make sure Selma was listening. "I'm going to lead an ordinary life for years—have children, do charities, and then, when I'm forty or fifty . . . I'll run off to the Orient and do something wicked . . . take for a lover a six-fingered Mongolian with a thing the size of a . . ." Metaphors failed. Joy described dimensions in the air with her hands and watched Selma's face clear and the laugh begin.

"Oh, la!" crowed Selma in the old way.

"How's that for a transaction?"

View from the Good Life

When she finally left Selma, Joy was already late, and it was blocks before she sighted a cab. She had the driver drop her at the corner market, picked up a small roast and a copy of *Time*, and climbed the hill to their apartment house.

Yin, the uniformed doorman, held the door for her.

"Beautiful day, Missy, no?"

"Beautiful day, yes."

Yin's obsequious style was a sham. He owned real estate all over the city and could buy and sell half the occupants of the building he served. Still he went on bowing and scraping with a sly interior smile that could almost be detected.

Yin made a formal presentation of their mail and escorted her to the elevator.

Most of the inhabitants of the place were elderly

widows, once wealthy, now suffering the shabby afflic-
tions of a fixed income in a time of inflation. They lived
under the shadow of a pathological fear that the owner
of the building, also an elderly widow, would desert
them: would either raise the rents herself or die and leave
the place to someone else who would raise the rents. For
entertainment the ladies had bridge and a proprietary
curiosity about "their" young people, Rolf and Joy. The
widows attempted the most amusing conversational ruses
to discover where their money came from and how much
of it there was.

There was a fair amount of it, but they were spending
it rapidly. Rolf said not to worry—yet. It came from two
strokes of luck: Rolf's promotion to the west coast office of his law firm and his sudden killing on the stock
market six months ago.

Joy liked to tease Rolf by saying that she'd married
him for his money. There was some truth to the gibe. Six
months ago, for reasons known only to himself, Rolf offered her the world and because she was frightened of
seepage and tired of dispossession, she took it.

She closed the apartment door after her and tripped
the two locks. Although their building had been immune
so far, there was an epidemic of breaking and entering in
the immediate neighborhood.

She walked through the living room and dining room
on her way to the kitchen, thinking—my things, my
things.

Sensing that for reasons he was not expected to appre-
hend furniture was important to her, Rolf had given her
a free hand in the matter. The rooms were large and

could accommodate the dark, massive, nineteenth-century pieces reminiscent of the furnishings in her father's house.

Now she no longer dreamt of the house, and now she understood that ownership was not a fact but an emotion—deep and potentially dangerous. It was not that she would ever kill for her possessions; rather, it was that suddenly she could imagine killing for them.

Once the roast was in, she took the mail to the spare room. It was as yet unfurnished and contained only two card tables and three large aquariums. She switched on the long fluorescent light above the tanks and the fish swam to the surface, hoping to be fed. That was Rolf's sacred province. As an acolyte she was allowed only the rite of the light—at precisely five in the afternoon.

Between five and five-thirty she usually devoted herself to the long-ledger. It was again a valuable companion. She cleared a space on a card table, pushing aside the complimentary copy of an obscure Canadian quarterly in which Zac had finally managed to get his story published. Although she wondered how the story ended, she had not yet got beyond *The basement flat had but one window.*

Slapping *Time* down on top of the lady poet (dog-eared, but also still unread), she flipped through the day's mail and separated bills from ads. A note from her father was the only thing of interest.

She read it through twice.

The widow had taken the bull by the horns—Cousin Patricia guffawed in the distance—and demanded a reckless elopement. They were married. It was a measure of

her father's devotion that he had consented to do anything during the middle of a semester. As a primitive
man might have been governed by the equinoxes, so he
was governed by the semesters. Things were done at the
beginning or end of a semester—never in the middle.

On a postcard she wrote just the last part of the first
proverb: *In winter enjoy,* and addressed it to him. She
fingered her father's note, then gazed at Stephen's paintings of the peak in *Time,* and finally defeated the moment's desolation by opening the long-ledger.

In past weeks it had become a very orderly document
Each day she recorded the date, the *Chronicle* headlines,
what she had bought for the apartment, and the condition of Selma.

October 2

QUAKES HIT BAY AREA

*Ordered from Magnin's: One chest of drawers with Sand-
wich glass knobs.*

Selma: Down and almost out. I pulled her up just in time.

Joy hesitated. then added another sentence. *Father is
married.*

At exactly five-thirty she closed the long-ledger, thinking for the thousandth time that her capacity for a sched-
ule and the fact that she enjoyed it so was astonishing.
Rolf insisted upon one. He was as stable as a battleship
towing with guys a dinghy in its wake.

Yes, it was good . . . better than either of them had
expected it could be . . .

Patricia slouched in front of the card table. "Dig the

chick with the chain in her hand, and at the end of the chain, the swinging world. Watch the world swing the chain and the chick."

Joy returned to the kitchen to mix and chill the cocktails, then arranged glasses and crackers and cheese in the living room. On the rosewood sofa there sat a panda with beautiful eyes bought for Anna; however, Joy was of two minds about sending it. For one thing, it was conceivable that Anna might already have passed beyond the meager consolations of stuffed animals; for another, to remember one of the children and not the others . . .

Three short rings meant Rolf.

She unlocked the door for him.

He put his arms around her and his hands renewed their knowledge of her. He liked to think of Joy and himself as high up, locked in alone—very large and enduring in a world of small distant things. He liked to think that nothing was so important as the extraordinary silent adventure between them.

"Guess what?"

"What?"

"Father's already married."

"So he went ahead and did it."

"Yes."

"Well, good for him. It's the best of all possible worlds, you know. Something smells good."

"Get yourself washed. Drinks are ready."

When they were settled, she said hesitantly, "Stephen ghosted me again today."

"Oh?" Although he urged her to feel free to talk about

the past, secretly he wished she'd just let it ride, leave it alone, put it away.

She passed him a magazine. He read the article she pointed to.

"Neoplatonist!" he roared. "That's got to be the fanciest euphemism for an acid head there ever was."

"Be fair," she said quietly. "He'd given all that up. Still, I agree that the article is nonsensical . . . his father's doing. Odious man. Nevertheless, I'm happy about the paintings—that they're being shown, even though I never liked them."

He watched her eyes instinctively seek the painting in a gilt frame hanging in a corner of the room—the painting of a lake with mountains in the background.

"I was a silly fool then . . . jealous of a mountain, can you imagine?"

"Yes, I can imagine. I'm jealous of your ghost."

"Don't be. It's over."

Rolf finished his drink, kissed her forehead, and went to feed his fish. He was especially concerned about the adjustment of a pair of new bettas to the tank. Fighting fish were a very complicated species. One couldn't be too careful.

The fish were at home. Easefully, they flicked in and out of the underwater shrubs.

Rolf brought a mirror to the side of the tank and held it there until the male fish caught sight of himself. His colorful fins spread, flashed; he attacked the glass.

During dinner they exchanged their days. Rolf confessed that he was sometimes perplexed by the problems of corporate tax; Joy confessed that she was sometimes per-plexed by the problems of Selma.

"If she'd just be sensible for a change," Rolf said, "if she'd just really let us do something to help. We can get her the best doctors in S.F., find out what's wrong with her, and have it taken care of."

"She won't. She's stubborn. She likes to be on her own."

They were silent, both solacing themselves—thinking that although they were ineffectual, at least they were well intentioned.

Rolf stood, stretched, and loosened his belt a notch.

He looked at himself in the mirror over the sideboard. "You're much too good a cook. I'm going to have to give up lunch."

Joy scowled over *Time* and turned the page—from the war to what was up in Czechoslovakia. Things were still bad there.

Yawning and rubbing his eyes, Rolf came in from the spare room where he had been working.

"Tired?"

"Hm." He went into the hall and double-locked the door.

"Rolf . . . do you ever get the feeling we're just waiting . . ."

He grabbed *Time* from her and flung it across the room. "The female mind . . . imaginary fog."

"Mating and waiting," she clowned. Sometimes her rhymes amused him.

Rolf turned off the lights, drew open the drapes, and

pulled up the blind. Together they stood at the window, watching a red bus inch up their hill under the clear October constellations: Gemini to the east, Cygnus to the west, Cassiopeia directly overhead.

"The paper says an inversion is likely within the next couple of days."

"Then the fog will be real."

"Yes, it will mean the end of our good weather."

"I wonder if the building will shake again tonight."

"Chances are against it. There's really nothing to worry about tonight. What time is it?"

"Late."

He brushed his fingers through her hair. She moved into the shelter of his arm.

Later Joy dreamt of the peak. Beyond a snowfield it towered in sunlight. She began the difficult traverse, the slow ascent.

28

Due 28 Days From Latest Date

AUG 3 0 1978			
OCT 1 1979			
		WITHDRAWN